THE MOORINGS OF MACKEREL SKY

A Novel by MZ

HYPERION AVENUE

LOS ANGELES • NEW YORK

First Edition, February 2024
10 9 8 7 6 5 4 3 2 1
FAC-004510-23348
Printed in the United States of America

This book is set in Hoefler Text
Designed by Stephanie Sumulong
Illustrations by Holly Ovenden

Library of Congress Cataloging-in-Publication Control Number:
2023014342
ISBN 978-1-368-09726-0
Reinforced binding

www.HyperionAvenueBooks.com

Logo Applies to Text Stock Only

All my love to

My wonderful parents, Carol and Tom,
their love and support my moorings;

My beautiful, brilliant daughters, Saoirse and Eowyn,
the wind in my sails;

My husband, Bruce, my North Star, all is love,
thanks for messing up my warm-up.

The Angler's Prayer

Lord give me grace
To catch a fish
So big that even I
When telling of it afterward
May never need to lie

Quand le mystère est trop impressionnant,
on n'ose pas désobéir.

—Antoine de Saint-Exupéry, *Le Petit Prince*

QUILT OF CONTENTS

Catastrophic Art

*L*eo Beale came from shit stock.

That was what everyone down at the IGA whispered buying bologna and white bread and coffee brandy. No one was
sure who Leo's father was, including his mother. There were
rumors: The father was her high school gym teacher, or in
the coast guard and got crabs testing the local waters; he
was her uncle. He might have been that Ellsworth boy who
dealt Oxys to all the fishermen one summer and overdosed
in a Bangor hotel room from a bad batch of black tar heroin.

Whoever his father was, he was gone, he was nameless, and Leo hoped he was dead.

Leo's mother was called Poppy, her real name forgotten. Her body was a temple for opiates, where her disciples worshipped in bliss and died cell by cell. She popped pills, spending her life in various states of semiconsciousness, skirting overdoses like skating on a pond in March, a constant state of flatlined emotion.

She never remembered her son.

Shit stock, they said, culled up from the dregs of the bait barrels, from the stink of the docks and the wet and the deep. Therefore, the grocery store gossips were not overly surprised that Leo tried to steal the car, or that he crashed it, or that he was drunk.

Leo was just barely three days turned thirteen. He lived on either point of the crescent of that age, at times the oldest thirteen-year-old ever and at times the youngest. He attended school enough to not be considered truant, but most teachers looked at him sadly and considered him a lost cause. Leo cared about school and liked it just fine, but in terms of his needs, it fell to about ninth place long after food and a warm bed.

People in the Maine town of Mackerel Sky oscillated between not believing someone that young could and would steal a car and wondering how long Leo had known how to drive, and if he had stolen something before. Possibly as long as four summers was the consensus—he had probably learned to drive illegally on the dirt roads of the blueberry barrens like most kids. But driving drunk is a catastrophic art, and Leo didn't have anywhere near the experience behind the wheel to try to fake driving well enough to drive anywhere plastered on coffee brandy, and his decision to steal Mrs. Myra Kelley's car and back it out of her barn was a trifecta of stupidity: First, he was reckless drunk when he did it, the drunk where his head hung heavy and waves of nausea pulled him into the riptide of the spins. Second, the Kelleys' barn was never meant to be a garage; it was converted, and the Alley boys from the island had done a shoddy, quick job of it, so even on a good, clear day with a good, clear head it was tricky to back out of the garage's mouth without clipping a mirror. And third, the driveway was icy; so, if that boy held a split-second spark of drunk-driving luck that night, the black ice snuffed it out and then froze it over.

Why Myra Kelley's car? Sometimes crime is the perfect chaotic concoction of opportunity and foolish fuel, and Leo was stumbling home drunk and cold, and her car was sitting in the garage, keys in the ignition. Myra had trouble seeing like she used to, and one day when she forgot her glasses and fully ran over her mailbox, flattened it flush with the flora, she parked her Buick in her barn-garage with the keys in it and left it there. That was five years ago. Myra had enough of driving and never did it again. Leo lived a couple miles around the corner from Myra, and he and his friends used to snowmobile on the trails and on the duck pond beside

Myra's house. He had explored the abandoned car with his wharf rat friends on occasions before this.

That night he stole it mainly because it was there and the coffee brandy insisted it was a brilliant idea. A lot of townspeople were surprised that the cold car even started up, including Leo, and Myra, who was asleep in her favorite armchair with her favorite winter-warmers—chamomile, her afghan, and her dog—when she heard the unfamiliar growl of the dormant engine. She jumped up and immediately got her good wooden broom, alerting her dog to a chase, his tail swishing in time with Myra's march out the front door.

The engine was still on, the car parked at a broken angle, its left side smashed into the mouth of the barn, the doors hanging on like loose teeth. The rear end had bumped into Myra's old maple tree. The driver had escaped out the open passenger door, as the driver-side door was pinned closed by a barn beam. Myra climbed in the passenger side, took the keys, and threw them in the snowbank. (Which in hindsight was not the smartest plan, but she was good and mad, and still had no plans of driving that car again. And, she'd make the boy find them later.)

Then she went out into the night, brandishing her broom like a pitchfork.

Myra Kelley saw where he was going and followed, despite the dark and the wet-cold of March and the fact he was three sheets to the wind. Residents of Mackerel Sky used the Paths, a series of foot-worn ruts that crisscrossed the town like lattice on a pie, settling over the established routes of labeled roads subtly, like a spiderweb on grass. To the right of Myra Kelley's porch, after her dog's tether, was one of the entrances to this series of ancient walkways through the woods and along the shore, and the Kelleys' tributary was well-worn, tread deep, its footfalls pounded in over hundreds of years. It went down a craggy rock ledge where her husband, Bernie, had planted hens and chicks one summer, and then cut through a lupine field. The boy tore off in that direction, and Myra Kelley followed.

Myra Kelley's trail was the quickest way down under the hill, and in winter, when the snowdrifts reached waist high, it was the only way down the hill. Myra and Bernie had kept the track well salted and sanded, and, strangely, snows on the foot routes always melted away a bit quicker there than everywhere else. Now it was just Myra tending it, and the weight of the salt was murder on her back.

But Myra Kelley knew the importance of maintaining the integrity of the Paths.

She did not shirk her duty, even when her husband had to up and get cancer and leave her alone to deal with the heavy bag of salt and apparently also stupid punks who couldn't drive cars out of barns. And chickens. Bernie's mother-cluck-clucking-stupid chickens. Myra stumbled, in part because it was night and black and icy, and in part because the chickens were loose and underfoot clucking up a cacophony, because Leo had also bumped their coop with the car.

The Kelley path led down the hill to the Perles' driveway and picked up across the road, ending at the tip of the tide. The boy would then take the road. The road split at the arc of the bay and peeled right and left around a beloved beach known as the Crescent. At either endpoint of the beach a tourist could jump into the sea; one side just hurt more than the other.

Myra would have guessed the boy would go left, and she would have assumed correctly, but if her chase had come down to whimsy and foolish guessing, Myra would have stopped and turned on her heel to head home; she was too levelheaded to chase this boy dang all over Creation. But as no-nonsense as she was, she couldn't just leave him. She had seen the car crash and seen a boy, and those were two things she couldn't close her eyes against.

In the distance she saw the boy puking brown foam into a snowbank. She picked up her pace. Leo saw Myra and ran again, which began the unexpected chase of Leo Beale by Myra Kelley all the way to the Aerie and High Cliffs.

The night was by no means warm, but after four solid months of winter cooling one's blood, freezing felt balmy, and with the high, full moon and no wind, the weather was tricky and dangerous—a short walk in a sweatshirt would leave you stupider and colder, a long walk might leave you dead. Myra Kelley added a caveat about appropriate winter dress to the internal speech she was preparing to deliver to the boy once she cornered him. He should not be out wearing nothing but a Pats sweatshirt.

Myra hadn't meant to follow him all the way to High Cliffs, but the boy's drunken pace perfectly matched her aged one so that he was always just close enough, bait to fish. Had people been looking out the windows instead of at their television sets they would have seen this strange nighttime parade, but most were content at their hearths, or dead asleep in their beds if they were fishing in the morning. Myra called the sheriff on her cell, but reception on the Cliffs was spotty, so although the sheriff got none of the content of the message, he got the identification of the caller. He knew Mrs. Kelley to be loud and foulmouthed at times, but she was no liar or attention seeker, so he put on his hat and headed out the door.

Leo was en route to one of the tips of the Crescent's points, High Cliffs and Burrbank's Aerie, a favorite stop of tourists in Mackerel Sky, who stood as close to the edge as they dared. Each side of the swollen arc that was the great Crescent Beach evolved into a new landscape that ended in cliffs: on the right end, the beach disappeared into boulders, covered in periwinkles and seaweed, shaded by the tree trunk posts of the piers of the Lone Docks and the port, and then ultimately faded into dunes; on the left side, the sands merged with rock and glacial remains, and disappeared into a cave below High Cliffs, which was breathtaking in both its majesty and its danger. A fall from High Cliffs meant certain death.

Although Leo came from shit history, and was careening toward High Cliffs at a steady clip, he wasn't suicidal. He was just drunk-running and pot-valiant and confused as all hell as to how his night ended up here, with Myra Kelley and her giant gray dog chasing him on the Paths with her broom.

But then he remembered. His mother.

It always came back to his drugged-out, pathetic excuse for a mother—high, high, always high—and the steady stream of men that swam in her swamp for varying lengths of months, each more miserable than the one before. Leo categorized them by single letters, and this month was D. D for drunk. D for dick. D for douche. Leo stole booze from him a lot, and that was all D was good for.

But now D had to go. He had split Poppy's lip for the second time, and though Poppy was an addict, and was bleary-eyed and drooling, and forgot that her son needed things like breakfast cereal and Band-Aids and dentist appointments, she was a human and female and his mom, and all of those things rang an internal alarm of *NO!* in Leo's heart, so Leo stood the tallest he could at thirteen, stood up to the encroaching D mountain of cigarette smoke and sweat and struggling organs and vile, and got punched in the face and in the ribs for it. His mother passed out on the couch. The next day she told everyone she tripped on the rug and smashed face-first into the coffee table, shattering the glass. Such was the extent of her injuries. And, Poppy wasn't lying. She didn't remember.

D had three bottles of Allen's coffee brandy, brown sugar

swill that he mixed with Moxie or cream or pulled from the bottle first thing when he woke up. Now, thanks to Leo, D, fortunately passed out and unaware, had a half of one bottle left, and it was gone. One shattered and sparkled on the snow and under the moon. One was shared with Leo and his fellow wharf rats, friends at the docks. The last bottle bounced around in Leo's sweatshirt pocket, half-empty.

The High Cliffs jutted over the ocean like an overbite, like an open mouth about to suck up the sea. At the bottom of the cliff was a cave known as Mermaid's Mouth, which grew and shrunk in size depending on the tides and tempests. Crescent Beach began in the throat of Mermaid's Mouth and stretched in an arc all the way to the last Lone Dock, black and cursed. The beach was accessible from High Cliffs only by a rambling wooden staircase haphazardly anchored to the rock, like a gardener trying to tamp an unruly vine. This was one of the oldest tributaries of the Paths. The Crescent, a beach with a haunting history, was swallowed whole by the deep at high tide. Tonight there was no sand at all, only the black of the ocean at night.

This time of year the staircase was long closed, though maintenance kept it clear of snow and ice. When Leo arrived at the staircase's locked gate he momentarily smartened up. He was drunk, but he wasn't going to try to go down those steps in winter, especially if Myra Kelley was going to keep following him. Every generation had a cautionary tale regarding the staircase at High Cliffs, and the most recent tragedy was only five years ago, when some Texas tourist tried to stretch over the edge to get a picture of a bald eagle. He slipped, and his body smashed and cracked down the steps all the way to the bottom, where he broke like a wave on the beach at the rictus of Mermaid's Mouth.

At least that is what Leo told himself later, that he would never be dumb enough to try to escape down those treacherous steps during the Ides of March. In reality he stopped running because he got viciously sick and threw up again on his knees in the snow. That's how Myra caught him, no coat, no hat, no gloves, a thin sweatshirt, throwing up all over himself in a snowbank at the gate of the staircase at High Cliffs. Myra's dog stopped between the boy and the edge.

"Jesus, kid. It smells like a trough at a pig bar."

Leo was heaving, sobbing, vomiting, his back arching. His T-shirt and sweatshirt rode up, exposing his skinny back, his ribs, his moles, his bruises from his mother's new boyfriend, his young age. Myra gritted her teeth at the angry welts, exhaled sharply through flared nostrils, and drove her broom into the snowbank like a stake. Myra never had babies that lived longer than a few months, but her sister did, so she knew how to handle a vomiting, retching child.

Poor, stupid boy.

She knelt next to him in the snow, pulled down his sweatshirt, rubbed him on the back, careful to avoid the bruising, and forgot completely about the Buick and the barn.

A bit out in the ocean sat Nimuë's Perch, a flat outcropping of rock that emerged as the tide receded. One of the many mermaid tales of Mackerel Sky had a story with these rocks as the setting—supposedly, they were where the great sea captain Burrbank first saw the mermaid Nimuë. He fell so in love with her that he built a temporary shelter on the Aerie so that he could forever gaze upon her beauty.

The town grew out of Burrbank's shelter and became Mackerel Sky.

This night, Nimuë's Perch was only a lone flat rock in an angry sea, steady black against a mottled ocean with waves like rows of teeth.

The boy threw up again. The coffee brandy fell out of his pocket; Myra flung it out into the sea.

"Land sakes and bilge cocktails! Coffee brandy, I see. Not as sweet on the way out, is it, kid?"

Myra didn't drink. She'd seen more than enough people commit suicide slowly with liquor, and at this age she was becoming forgetful enough; she didn't need to speed up the process with booze. Clearly this boy was not worried about the effects of alcohol on the brain. She felt the ice of legitimate worry when the boy began to shake and when the vomiting wouldn't stop.

Suddenly the moon came out from behind a cloud and split the dark of the night in a seam. Myra looked up.

A mermaid lounged on Nimuë's Perch, a prow of everything lush and ferocious, wet eyes fixed on Myra and Leo. In her spotlight of moonlight she tilted her head to the side, a wave followed, crashing flirtatiously in response. Her tail, silver and pearl, light reflecting off it like an oil slick, furled, beckoning.

Myra and the mermaid stared coldly at each other for a moment, and then Myra nodded her head once. Leo, a blubbering mess of snot and vomit, wiped his face on Myra's sleeve and followed her line of sight. The mermaid's sharp black eyes focused on the boy. She raised one palm and lifted one finger, and drew all the alcohol out of him like the moon pulled the tide. The mermaid then slipped under the waves.

After a deluge of sweat, tears, vomit, and piss, Leo blinked, and settled into his sudden sobriety with a hiccup. These were his thoughts:

I am on the Cliffs. I puked on Miss Myra. I might have killed one of her stupid chickens. I can't tell if I am drunk or sober. I think I am sober. I don't know how.

I can't be sober. I drank it all, to the dregs. I can't be sober.

I just saw a real live mermaid.

I should be dead.

Then he passed out.

Edge of Man

*M*ostly, change came to Mackerel Sky at the same pace rock crumbled to sand. Gradually, the great stone cliff giants who bore the violence of the waves disintegrated into beach, but a resident never saw it in their lifetime. For a long time the locals had been reticent about accepting the big-*G* Gay; for a long time the locals felt about homosexuals the same way they felt about tornadoes: they were a rare sight, native to other lands. But cracks of acceptance had begun slicing veins in the rocks in the foundation of Mackerel Sky, like quartz, clear, sparkling.

Derrick Stowe split the foundation in two.

Derrick sat near Leo in Mrs. Perle's writing class. Leo couldn't write the poem about his family, even with the product descriptor. He was really hungry, and he got stuck with where to put the comma:

> *I have a mother, who is high, all the time.*
> *I have a mother who is high, all the time.*
> *I have a mother who is high all the time.*
> *#Ihaveamotherwshoishighallthetime*

He would never turn it in to Mrs. Perle. He'd prefer to pass nothing in and fail.

Derrick wrote:

> *Help me, Atargatis, for I am told to stay away from*
> *God's dick.*

He then chewed on his pen, very thoughtfully.

It was a beautiful thing, first good love. Ricky Townsend, a boy, edge of man, unsure, cocksure, and life was full and open. At sixteen Ricky fell stone-sunk in love with the star pitcher of his baseball team, Derrick Stowe, for all the reasons one falls in love with the star pitcher of the baseball team: he was gorgeous, kind-hearted, tall, honest, and hopeful, and you could trust that bastard with a ball and a bat. Derrick Stowe fell in love right back with the soulful big-eyed and big-lipped dreamer. And for a long time neither knew and neither told the other.

Derrick only had three real thoughts when he realized he was in love with Ricky Townsend—first, *oh*, and then *shit*, and finally *I'll eventually need to tell my dad*. Derrick sometimes smiled shyly at Ricky. But he said or did nothing else, and that was that for a while.

Until Ricky began smiling back that October. And that moment in the car in late December after they catapulted the Christmas Pig and became lovers in secret.

After school Derrick walked his dog, Duke, a fluffy beast, a golden retriever, along the Crescent, the sand webbed in between the fingers of High Cliffs and the Lone Docks on Low Cliffs. Duke dug in the sand and swam in the surf like it was summer always. He had terrible breath and always smelled like bait, and his favorite pastime was rolling in dead things, but he carried all of Derrick's secrets. Duke chased after Derrick's rocks, his practice pitches, flung far into the ocean, each rock followed by a comet of Derrick's lamentations: why, why love had to be so complicated, why he had to be gay, why his mother had to drown.

Derrick liked to look for things forgotten in the sea. He combed through what the swells belched and shed. He found a black Converse sneaker converted into a condominium for mussels, a pair of Oakleys missing a lens, and so many pieces of boats. He wasn't sure what he was looking for exactly; he was intrigued by what the sea stole and what it returned. He couldn't decide if debris that floated back to shore had been deemed worthy or unworthy.

He'd heard the tales of Nimuë and her mermaids, and how they lured New England sailors into the ocean through song, through seduction, through the infinite chasm of love. The sailors, enchanted, fell in love with the sirens, the unlucky ones were drowned, and then forever floated as statues in the underwater cities of the mermaids, kelp tethering them to the ground, embalmed tributes to strangeness and youth and eternal love.

Derrick grew up under his mother's skirts in the Millcreek Library on a happy leash of stories. His mother worked there for the entire eight years she lived in Mackerel Sky, before, after, and during her pregnancy. Derrick never knew a time without the depths of books. He remembered flurries of kindness in the form of old ladies from the church and the triad of women known as the Three Bats, who had worked at the library until their dear old bodies retired them to rocking chairs at the wharf's edge. Widow Adelaide Pines worked there the longest, and worked there still—"a rock in the land," Myra Kelley would say—and was a living search engine, Google before Google was invented. After his mother died, Derrick kept returning to the library at her scheduled work times (before school every day and after school on Thursdays), and Widow Pines and the old ladies took care of him, and, when he declared himself a man at nine, they gave him work. On Thursday afternoons he read three books for story time: one the group voted on, one he chose, and one chapter of a chapter book. The hour was supposed to be for kids only (or BOYS ONLY, the first sign he made), but anyone from the town might show up. Often ruddy-nosed lobsterman Deaddeer would show up right from the boat with his granddaughter and then promptly take a nap, though never before he participated in the vote. After the stories were read, Widow Pines would sit and spin a yarn about the mermaid mythos of Mackerel Sky, how Captain Burrbank and Nimuë the Mermaid fell in love, and how Mackerel Sky was prosperous under Burrbank's cunning leadership and the mermaids' favor, until the townspeople betrayed the mermaids three times, and the town was cursed.

The library was an abandoned mill on what was once a river more wild. It became a library by wind. A hurricane whipped up the coast and beat it mercilessly, flattening towns and splintering boats. One captain of one of these battered boats had two lifeboats, and he put all his men in one and himself and his books in the other. The men mostly survived; the books survived, but the captain did not. The books floated upriver to the abandoned mill and stayed there, and the Millcreek Library was born.

Derrick adored the mermaid legends of Mackerel Sky as much as he adored the library. He liked that they gave his town depth and history, the belief that under the day-to-day there was something more. His father called that God. Derrick didn't know about God, because according to most churchgoers on the coast God hated gays, but he liked reading about Captain Burrbank's crew: the man who carried a monkey, a Congolese first mate who was only referred to as the Dark Terror in the Night, the Tattooed Twins, the captive Esmeralda, who they called the Piratebird, and the great Captain Ichabod Burrbank, who tamed the seas and the mermaids within.

Before she died, his mother had been recording the town's nautical history and lore. She spent hours in the library and by the sea scratching in her notebooks. After she drowned, Derrick found her again in her handwriting and her doodles in the annals of her journals, where she had taken notes and written histories over the years.

She wrote of Burrbank's first mermaid encounter:

The sight of a merrow means an incoming gale, and mermaid sightings had been sluicing through the fog for days. The men were on edge. The Dark Terror had taken to drinking from two jugs in the rhythm of the waves. Some of the crew had sworn they had seen her, the siren, sworn she was calling to them, sworn they would never be the same.

In the cold white fog of morning bare-breasted she lay, ivory bust of tantalizing softness, on her back, playing with a fishing net, rocking on a wave. She lounged on a makeshift raft, a bite of fallen ship, a previous prey, stranger-comrades whom the mermaids had drowned.

Two.

Two days.

Two days of no wind, the air fog and sickly gray.

Two.

Two men.

Two men, seasoned, veterans of the sea, had disappeared into the drink.

Town legend said that Mackerel Sky grew from the lean-to that Captain Burrbank built on High Cliffs in order to search for his mermaid love. Now on High Cliffs rested a simple monument, a stone menhir with a plaque that read in no-nonsense Maine fashion, 1711—WHERE THE CAPTAIN SAW THE MERMAID. That spot on top of High Cliffs was called Burrbank's Aerie, and tourists hiked there during the summer to glimpse Nimuë's Perch, a rock that was only visible during low tide, the rock where Captain Burrbank purportedly spotted Nimuë the Mermaid and fell helplessly in love. A bald eagle christened Maximus had claimed the cove as his own, and sometimes he was seen soaring overhead, his screeches echoing through time.

Supposedly, after Captain Burrbank first stood on the cliff and glimpsed the Mermaid, he kept a night vigil under the brightest stars of the Aerie, waiting to see his love.

When he waited longer than one night, he built a shelter. When he waited longer than one month, he built a town. Younger then, the bustling coast needed a mid-port on the newer, Northeastern trade routes, and Mackerel Sky was ideal—welcoming, beautiful, beckoning the lost and the remote. Younger then, Burrbank lived like a current and only disembarked when the ocean willed it. Ironically, Nimuë, the creature married to the ocean, was the reason Burrbank finally put down roots, first to be with her, then to be rid of her.

At the base of High Cliffs, far below the Aerie and the widespread wings of Maximus, the ocean dug away at the cave known as Mermaid's Mouth, and with the cave's innards created Crescent Beach. Derrick's classmates had bonfires at the mouth of the cave all the time, and if a kid could navigate the edge of the ocean, the cliffs, the wooden steps, the night, and the honeypots, drunk, he had a good time.

Derrick didn't enjoy the bonfires as much as most of his high school friends; he didn't really drink, and alcohol around water made him anxious. But he went, because that was what you did on the weekends in high school. Derrick lived on the outskirts of popularity like a trend. When it was baseball season and he pitched, because he could paint the corners better than anyone else, the students hailed him and called him Rembrandt. But the rest of the year, when he disappeared into the library or on his father's boat to haul, he was just Derrick, and whispers of his sexuality orbited him.

Fortunately the whispers had stayed as such and had yet to reach his father.

Derrick's father was one of the few Black men in town, an incredibly tall blade of lean muscle and a human extension of boat. Some men were born to balance on wooden planks in the middle of punishing swells, and Stéphane Stowe was one of them. After his wife, Millie, drowned, Stéphane turned hard as stone and lobstered the ocean with reckless, fearless grief, a rock against the waves, challenging them to break him down to sand.

Millie had written:

Mermaids are, of course, most drawn to water, but water in any form, including water in the body. That is why they were initially attracted to humans, sailors and pirates and explorers, due to proximity. Mermaids circled ships of drunk seamen; they were easy prey. Water is magnetic to mermaids.

They are also as much treasure hunters as pirates, and search the reefs and shoals for nacre jewels, none more valuable to the merrow than the pearl.

Derrick wanted to believe wholeheartedly in the existence of mermaids, but he had never seen one anywhere but in his dreams, and he was getting to the age where adulthood required that he forget legends and magic. Besides, believing in mermaids was really, really gay, and right now the gossip regarding his sexuality was nothing but mere rumors, easily swatted away and destroyed like spiderwebs with a laugh or wink at one of the girls, even destroyed for weeks when he pitched a no-hitter, so he didn't ever want to add fuel.

Also, finally, his mother was the one who had believed in mermaids, and she was long dead. He should move on.

Derrick sat in Mrs. Perle's creative writing class next to Ricky, glancing at him side-eyed. The end of the day and Friday, class almost over, no one was working, and Mrs. Perle kept shushing them to the point that Arnie, a thick-necked senior, stood up and told everyone to settle down for Mrs. Perle in his best teacher voice.

They did too; Ricky swallowed his smile, and Derrick swatted him with his notebook, earning an eyebrow from Mrs. Perle. No one in the public schools gave any shit to Mrs. Perle, on account she had gone crazy and all. The Fourth of July and Mermaid Festival fireworks didn't even go off the year her baby died. Actually, the fireworks didn't go off because the fog rolled in like it did most years, but Myra Kelley said (and everyone agreed) that that year God brought the fog in out of respect.

Derrick dropped his notebook on the floor and he and Ricky simultaneously reached to pick it up. Their fingers brushed together and stayed, just long enough. Just long enough for the couple of faggot haters in the class to notice, seethe, and bond in hate.

Red Sky at Morning

*M*rs. Manon Perle's school day as a teacher could be summed up in three thoughts:

1. There is not a nurse at the shelter. If there were one, she probably would not know the French word for migraine.

2. We are relieved and glad your son is at school, but he has lice again (or still). And, he has really big hair.

3. My daughter is dead in the sea.

When this final thought came in, unbidden, as it was wont to do, Manon always imagined her daughter as a mermaid, the sea different shades of green, its own forest of different darks, her daughter's hair like kelp. Those fantasies brought eyes to her hurricanes.

Before her daughter was born, Manon's favorite part of the town's mermaid legend was how Burrbank and Nimuë first embraced, underwater, as battle waged above on his ship, the *Bellaforte*. Burrbank, gouged in the gut by a saber and bleeding badly, had been tossed into the drink. Nimuë came upon him then as he floated down, a fog of blood billowing around him.

The mermaids had been dogging his boat, driving his men insane. Then the pirates came in the night. Burrbank had seen Nimuë in bits and glimpses, a tease of skin, pale like starlight, a flick of her tail, like lace, the curved indent of her lower back like a violin. Suddenly here she was, full and rapturous, as clear as he could see her through the weight of water. She kissed him, filling his mouth with her tongue and the salt sting of seawater. Then she exhaled deeply, and filled his burning lungs with hot air from her body. Manon loved that image, the *Mermaid's Kiss*, replicated many times by many artists, including Manon herself. She had stitched it as an image in her quilts repeatedly. Manon always imagined that when Nimuë first kissed Burrbank underwater, her flowing hair and tail curved around Burrbank like the arcs of a crescent moon.

They say then, when Burrbank crawled back from the dead and back over the side onto the deck, his crew rallied and defeated the pirates to save their ship. They set up their mooring off Mackerel Sky to rest and recover, and the next night Burrbank explored the land and found High Cliffs, and when he looked out and saw the mermaid that saved him lounging lusciously on her perch, he fell in love fully, completely.

Now, after her daughter was dead, Manon found that she preferred the last part of the legend, where, twenty years after he built the lean-to and founded Mackerel Sky, Burrbank walked away from everything and vanished off of High Cliffs. No one knew if he committed suicide, or jumped to be with his love, or boarded the next vessel and sailed away. That morning rose a sun weak but filtering through the clouds enough that it could to shine on the town in mourning. Manon liked this part of the legend, she liked to know that the world went on through tragedy and that she too could disappear, especially on days when she was stuck in her head in a memory on repeat, a memory where her hands went into the ocean holding her daughter and came out wet and empty.

Derrick Stowe wrote poetry in Manon Perle's creative writing class. He wrote:

> *Red sky at morning*
> *Sailors*
> *Take warning*
> *There are few maids upon the waves*

They have gone under
Tendrils of kelp and hair in their wake
A lone bird
Breaks into some phoenix's lament
If you hear it, sailors,
Notes to sky
Notes to ground
Heed it,
For they come

She enjoyed reading her students' work. Manon had only just returned to teaching this fall, after a three-year hiatus. She honestly hadn't thought she would ever return. She was originally an elementary school teacher, but Mackerel Sky only had one elementary school, and Manon could not bear to set foot under that roof again, with its smells of snack time and posters with sweet, stumbling script and echoes of little laughs, the school her daughter would not ever attend. So she was moved to the high school, and was put into a quiet-corner sort of position, one on the fringes of the mainstream so that if she fell into an all-consuming depression again she could easily be extracted. She taught creative writing as an elective to a mix of middle and high school students and was the Gifted and Talented liaison for the entire school system, programs that were luxuries in the mostly forgotten rural high schools on the coast, programs that ebbed and flowed with the budget tide.

Many days at work this winter she found herself staring into the snow, wondering what it would be like to be suffocated by white. When she saw ghosts reflected in the window, and storms whipped up internally like in the hollows of mountains, she turned away. She did some correcting, some planning, told off the Townsend twins in class for some foolishness or another, scraped off gum under desks with the edge of a ruler, anything to avoid remembering.

Winter in Mackerel Sky had many layers of quiet—snow like a muffling blanket, the streets during a snowstorm, freezing nights. Mornings before a blizzard, the sky sometimes ripped and bled where it met the ocean and a lovely layer of pink rose with the sun, the church steeple spires silhouetted by sunrise. If they were smart, mariners heeded and knew to avoid the water on those days.

Years ago, Manon's baby, Nimue, was breeching in this precious pink time before a blizzard, when the quiet was like all the world was holding its breath, when all the town marveled with a sparkle of fear at a pretty morning moment in defiance of the impending clouds. The week had been days and days of spitting and squalling snow, but the morning Jason and Manon Perle drove to the hospital to have their baby, the weather split like the Red Sea, an intake of breath between snows and storm. Manon would have preferred a home birth, but with a blizzard on the way and both of her midwives down with the flu, a home birth was clearly not in the cards. Jason was just fine driving to the hospital, thank you very much. It gave him something to do besides worry, for his life was in the passenger seat next to him and he'd rather they be surrounded by warmth, doctors, and walls. And Jason was a lobsterman with a few solid superstitions who knew how to read a sky.

If they had not gone, the baby and the mother would have died immediately. Manon would have bled out; her daughter would not have been able to breathe.

Her daughter had been born to die.

Manon thought about that, years and lifetimes later, and somehow it brought her comfort, knowing that nature would have taken mother and child together. She could have died with her daughter.

Since he was nine, Jason never had eyes for anyone else except for Manon. Before helicopter parents and helmets and iPads, they used to ride bikes in a pack of children all over the Paths, roaming Mackerel Sky like the coyotes that stalked the house cats. Jason's heart flopped over into Manon's lap after he took a digger on his bike and she bandaged his split knee with a wad of gum, and then proceeded to nail the jump that he had missed.

"You have to trust that the bike will be there," she told him, "and you can't ride the ramp on the left side; it's warped. Get a good line. Starting out wrong is not the way to start." She spat on the gum. "Try again."

He kept trying.

Manon and Jason Perle owned the house under the hill from

Myra Kelley, a wraparound cape with a big bay window that overlooked an inlet that changed with the tide. There they had fed a murder of crows out back and picked apples and picnicked on blankets on rock crags under the sun. Until it all fell apart, and Manon ended adrift in mental institutions for a time and Jason lobstered far out on the Atlantic, the days had been good.

Although she had moved out of that house over two years ago, Jason still owned it, and still left a key under a plant pot by the door for Manon, should she need it.

The night Nimue Perle was born, the power went out in the hospital. This happened so rarely that this historical fact became an irrefutable testament to the severity of the blizzard of '99. Maine hospitals don't black out for more than a blink, but in that blink Nimue Perle came into the world with a great gurgling scream. The power shut off, plunging the hospital into a black void, like a trench underwater. All the staff collectively paused in silence. Then, as lightning quickening the dead, the baby Nimue's first shrill cry snapped the staff out of their reverie and sent them scurrying to find light in the dark.

The generators kicked in and the lights flickered back on in Manon's room. She took deep, exhausted breaths, drenched in sweat and bleeding out the birth. The orderlies and the doctor had not started moving again; they stood transfixed at the warming table, stealing shocked glances at each other, and at all costs avoiding the eyes of the new parents, who were fortunately momentarily oblivious, relieved as they were. Jason was kissing Manon's wet eyelashes, and kept whispering, "You did so good, baby," over and over again. His truck was still parked next to the ambulance, hazards on, lights on, door closed on the seat-belt strap.

Nimue the baby, rosy and wailing. Nimue, the baby with a tuft of black hair poking out in pointed triangles. Nimue, the baby Jason and Manon would one day lose. Nimue the baby, named for Nimuë the Mermaid, who was so loved by Captain Burrbank that he founded Mackerel Sky.

Nimue the baby, their baby, had been born with sirenomelia, her body fused together from the waist down.

Outside the blizzard blanketed and the hospital lights flickered, and the seas raged high, full of frothy teeth.

A Gentleman's Agreement

*M*yra Kelley recognized a child raised by the wild when she saw one.

The jutting rib bones, the darting eyes, the crossed arms, the recoil. Hood up, slumped, in different circumstances Leo might look like a punk thug thirsting for a fight, but right now Leo was holding a bucket and looked entirely young and alone.

"Is that really necessary, Gerald?" She pointed to the cell; the sheriff shot Leo a sideways glance.

"Yessah. Sober him up right quick. He's only in there until his mom shows up anyway."

"We both know she isn't coming." She was done being angry about her car and her barn; now she just wanted to get back home. And take that foolish child with her to give him something to eat.

The sheriff didn't say anything, but his pencil had stopped. Leo puked.

"I'm not letting that boy sleep here no matter how fool-headed he is. He might have fallen off that cliff."

Myra's last name was originally Boucher, French Acadian. Her heritage was a motley mix of Acadians and Wabanaki, traders and sailors who settled on the coast of Maine. She was tough as rock salt. She was as bright as pine.

Some even said she descended from Burrbank and the Piratebird, but Myra Kelley never countenanced those rumors.

"I'll wait." She was still carrying her broom, and the loyal Dog sat next to her just as decisively. He was unlike any dog Leo had ever seen. He was a tall wiry horse of an animal with a snout that carried the distinguished frost of old age, and he stood at Myra's waist.

"I saw a goddamned mermaid, Miss Myra. Like Burrbank's mermaid. And, I ain't drunk no more, I swear it. I don't know how. She sucked it out of me, I swear. I'm hungover now. I'm never drinking again." He puked out the period on the end of his sentence.

"Good choice, kid." Myra and Sheriff Badger spoke synchronously.

"Mermaids, huh?" Sheriff Badger tapped his pen and looked directly at Myra.

"Just the one, he says." Leo didn't know if Myra was being serious or not, but the look the sheriff and the old lady shared was long and silent and tense.

"Glad you're sober, kid. You might be crazy, though. And watch your mouth," Sheriff Badger replied, put his hat on his head over his long braid and stood to unlock the cell, but then put his keys away. With a smile, he simply opened the door.

"Look at that. It was always unlocked." Sheriff Badger chuckled and shook his head.

At four in the morning the sheriff drove Myra and Leo back to Myra's, the boy asleep in the backseat, his head on the shoulder of Myra's sturdy frame. The dog sat in front with the sheriff like he was born to it. Leo's mother had been arrested for drunk and disorderly conduct in the parking lot of a Bangor bar and was sleeping it off in a cell out there. The light of the coming dawn was a hazy violet, framing the boats sitting silent in their slips. The boatyard had been awake for a while, the lobstermen setting out on the water.

As the car stopped, the sheriff tried once more. "You're sure, Myra? I still think you should press charges. You don't know this kid's coming back."

"I'll have him sign a gentleman's agreement." She punctuated the sentence with her broom. "It's fine, Gerald. I think fixing my barn is going to be a much better punishment than a permanent record, or one of those hellhole kid jails. Good morning to you." She opened the door and hit a chicken and cussed.

Myra Kelley lived in a mint-green clapboard house with a farmer's front porch framed by hydrangeas and holly, set on a small, scraggly hill dotted with clusters of blueberries. A blue cooler labeled KELLEY sat at the stoop. The hill overlooked a duck pond that froze over every winter. Leo had ice-skated (actually just slipped around the ice in his boots because he didn't own skates) and ridden on the back of a snowmobile on the frozen pond with the wharf rats there.

Her barn was out back behind the house and to the left, its mouth gaping open with the car hanging off the side like a cigar.

The chicken coop was busted up from the accident and would need fixing. The chickens were as contained as they could be on the front porch. Myra's late husband, Bernard Kelley Jr., loved hard-boiled eggs out on the boat, and in the twilight of his life had decided that he wanted to keep chickens. Unfortunately, shortly after he purchased twelve rambunctious chicks, cancer took him, and he never recovered. The chickens lived longer than he did, and they had been tripping up Myra's stride ever since.

Leo had trick-or-treated at Myra's house before. She gave out good candy. Her porch creaked, the screen door squeaked, but the light from inside was always golden and warm, and it always smelled like fried fish or bread baking, not like forgotten beer spills or sharp sweat like his trailer. Some of the kids said Myra Kelley was a witch.

When Leo stepped inside, Dog brushed past him to his food dish, nails clicking on the linoleum, and looked at Leo expectantly.

"Don't let Dog lie to you. He's already been fed."

Dog sat defiantly and nudged Leo's hand.

"See, he's a liar, and good at it too. I suspect you're tired. Let me show you where you can lay down, kid, and then I'll fix you something to eat."

The boy followed Myra to a room in the back of the house with windows facing the woods and the barn. On the bed was an exquisite quilt with nine panels, pictures of pirates and a shipwreck and mermaids and the sunrise, pictures orbiting the center where Burrbank and Nimuë embraced underwater in the famous Mermaid's Kiss. The quilt that covered the bed told the tale of the founding of Mackerel Sky.

Leo sat on the soft bed, the biggest and cleanest he had ever been on, and Myra went to fetch another afghan. When she returned, though, little Leo Beale was snoring on the pillow, and Dog was at his feet, his shaggy head resting on the boy's ankles. She covered him with two afghans that she had crocheted herself before retiring to her own bed, and they all slept deeply as the sun rose.

It wasn't until the early afternoon when Leo woke, Myra

fed him eggs and bacon and white toast and orange juice until he stopped eating (twelve eggs, six slices of toast slathered in butter, a half slab of bacon, and two and a half glasses), and then they discussed the terms of their agreement. But she would not discuss mermaids. Myra Kelley wouldn't have it, and Leo was thankful to not be in jail or his mother's trailer, so he shut his mouth.

Leo was to sell Myra's car to a junkyard ("It's far past time I get rid of that fossil"), clean out the barn, repair the chicken coop (or "pluck and roast every one of those damn little pains-in-the-ass"), and fix the barn. Myra had written it all up. He signed it easily, because the work was to begin in May, and being late March the work seemed forever away. Two months was a lifetime, especially in Poppy's trailer. Plus, Mrs. Myra had been really nice to him, and he wanted to mend what he had broken.

After their late breakfast, Myra handed him a tube of medicine. He struggled to read its name.

"Arnica," Myra explained. "It will help heal your bruises. I'm so, so sorry that happened to you, Leo boy." Myra said nothing more, but she had opened the conversational door, and Leo felt something akin to relief.

They went out to check out the barn and the chicken coop. Dog started barking, and a clunker roared up the driveway. Leo recognized it and shrunk; his shoulders hunched up like he was trying to retreat into his body like a turtle. The passenger door opened, and Leo flinched. Myra saw it all. She stood up straight, as straight as she could against the body furl of old age, and stepped between Leo and the car.

Poppy Beale stumbled out, high; her driver stayed smoking in the dark of the car. She didn't see them by the barn and so stalked and stumbled to the front door and banged loudly, flailing a lit cigarette around. Her clothes hung, her legs were skinny and bowed, her eyeshadow was dark and overdone. Her concealer did not conceal the drug decomposition. Myra called out to her. When Poppy saw Leo, she began yelling at him for stealing the brandy, for stealing the car, tweaking, twitching. Her words, a vile vitriol, an avalanche of grievances, what no mother should ever say to their child, were screeched with all the bravado and sense of a toddler until Myra Kelley had endured thirty whole seconds of the sound. Dog began growling and Myra Kelley swept the woman off of her porch with her broom. Poppy got back into the car and squealed off, abruptly, devastatingly, like an explosion.

"She smells like she's rotting," Leo stated, after his mother peeled off with D still smoking behind the wheel. His voice was flat, dull, defeated.

Myra stood soldier still, her hands on her housecoat on her hips, grinding her teeth. She was good and pissed.

"Nail on the head, boy."

If Myra still smoked, now she would have, but she didn't anymore, so she contented herself with chewing on the end of her husband's empty old pipe. It had sat on his dresser for months after he died, the sweet musk an instant bridge to memory. She imagined him with it now, leaning against the corner of the covered porch like he did, arms and legs crossed.

"She's a ripe bitch, ain't she, my Lorelei?" he would have said, the smoke punctuating the point. Myra chuckled under her breath at the memory and looked out at her front yard.

"See that tree over there? The one with the low-hanging branch?"

Leo looked up with red, red eyes. It was an apple tree.

"That branch right there, the long one in front, it didn't bear fruit for the longest time. I was going to cut it off for the good of the tree. Then one day my husband hammered in a nail at the branch's base, right through the heart of it. And since then, getting that extra iron, that branch has been the most fruitful of the whole tree."

"Miss Myra. I don't know what the hell you are talking about."

"Boy, watch your mouth. I'll wash it out with soap next time. Not this time," she added as a caveat, noting his round, wet eyes. "That's okay, kid, you don't have to know what I'm talking about. I do. It means that that mother of yours doesn't get to decide if you rot or if you bloom. Not on my goddamned porch."

Missing Words

Mermaids sing stories
to the moons at night
Waxing, waning, full
They learn secrets
from the stars
Tell me yours
boy
and I will tell you mine

… *W*rote Derrick in Mrs. Perle's creative writing block at the end of the day. She read it over his shoulder making her rounds in the classroom. He had read something about mermaids whispering to the stars in his mother's favorite journal once, a leather book with a big hole in the front like it was missing something inlaid. Unfortunately, when she died that journal had disappeared. He had other journals and writings of hers to comfort him, but he remembered that one specifically, and wanted to read those missing words. He had asked his father, but his father had no memory of it.

Manon did not want to read about mermaids today so she moved on.

"Why do you not want to talk about mermaids?" one of the psychiatrists at the sanatorium had asked her once.

"Because I gave my dead child to one," Manon had answered, arms wrapped around her knees. The psychiatrist was young, new, and did not have a question to follow up.

Manon and Jason named their baby after the most famous mermaid in New England: Nimuë of the Dark, Captain Burrbank's love, but they left off the accent tréma over the *e* because they thought it was a little too pretentious.

The most accessible story of Nimue's namesake was typed up on the place mats at the Mermaid's Tail Tavern, a restaurant set on the second of the Lone Docks. Fried catch and cole-slaw, underfoot the ocean through the wharf, the restaurant bulged like a summer tick June through September, and was boarded up during the off-season, boarded up during the blizzard Nimue was born.

Before they were covered in chowder rings and cobbler crumbs, the paper mats advertised local catch and mechanics and hairdressers and told "The Mermaid's Tale," the story of how Mackerel Sky was founded. Captain Ichabod Burrbank and his bonded crew, on the last leg of an adventure fraught with pirates and vicious seas and death, sailing north from the port burgeoning in Salem, after a pirate attack, marooned their ship, the *Bellaforte*, off High Cliffs and Crescent Beach. Supposedly that very night, under a web of starlight and a bulbous moon, Burrbank heard Nimuë's watery song and saw her lounging on her perch. He fell in love with her then and there, violently, obsessively, and vowed to remain until he saw her again. The town grew out of his vigil.

According to the mats in the booths of the Mermaid's Tail, for ten years the town flourished under Burrbank's rule and the blessing of the mermaids, until the Sea Captain and his people thrice betrayed the sirens. Under a blood moon Nimuë and her merrow brothers and sisters attacked the town of Mackerel Sky. "Torch Night," so named for all the fires lit by the residents and Wabanaki to threaten the mermaids, claimed the lives of eight residents of the town. The next morning Burrbank vowed to have nothing more to do with the sea or Nimuë. He remained in Mackerel Sky and developed it into a vibrant, prosperous trade port and lumber town. Ten years after Torch Night, under the heavy harvest moon, he vanished off of High Cliffs and was never seen again.

The Mermaid's Tail Tavern was itself well over two hundred years old, an iteration of the original mariners' dock pub, the Ink and Crane.

Some information was not mentioned on the Mermaid's

Tail place mats, was not shared with tourists. Most residents believed the town was still cursed to this day, their cited evidence the history of the town's steady train of sacrifices to the ocean. Jason Perle knew the exact number, but never shared it. It was an anchor that he carried alone.

Jason became president of the memorial chapter of the Mackerel Sky Community Committee (MSCC) the same week he became captain of his brother's lobster boat, a week where its beginning and its end were two entirely different lifetimes. The MSCC was in charge of all the social and community events in Mackerel Sky; they organized a myriad of things to keep the inhabitants of the tiny town entertained, such as the Fourth of July lobster-boat races, decorating contests during holidays, dances, pageants, and the lucrative three-day Mackerel Sky Mermaid Festival in August.

That week Jason had started out as a sternman. He had started that week lobstering part-time. He started out that week with a brother. He remembered loading up the boat with his brother and looking at the sky that morning—a pink seam spilt the horizon like sliced skin that spread and bled into a rose-gold sunrise. He didn't remember fishing that day, but he would never forget his brother's surprised shout, then a splash, then the search for him overboard. At skinny seventeen, Jason watched their dead dad's old drinking buddy known as Deaddeer pull his brother's body out of the water. Jason followed Deaddeer's boat back to port, the radio turned all the way up to drown out the silence that sat stubborn in the stern like a Down East fog.

The next week Jason dropped out of school and registered as the captain of his deceased brother's lobster boat. He then asked to join the memorial chapter, and as Deaddeer was the only other member and hated computers and paperwork and anything not related to fishing, Jason had taken it over almost as immediately as he arrived. He commissioned a sculpture on Low Cliffs, a beautiful maiden standing on a pedestal reaching for the sea, her dress and hair whipping in the wind, the virgin on the rocks, reminding the sailors to come home. Next to her was a great stone, where the names of the fallen had been etched into the rock. Burrbank's name fell about thirtieth (1731), and Vincent Perle, Jason's twenty-two-year-old brother, was etched well after the two thousand mark. Every Mermaid Festival in August Jason held a candlelight vigil for the lost residents of Mackerel Sky, a moment of silence, a song. He began it the year his brother died and had done it ever since. Every year he added names to the rock, the remains of a lifetime etched in letters and stone.

There was only one year he did not light candles to honor the dead, one year he could not attend the memorial, the summer his daughter died. That summer, during the Mermaid Festival, they left the wharf a tiny, happy family, and when they returned, when Manon Perle came off her husband's lobster boat that day in August, their only child, little Nimue Perle, was not only dead but missing, gone, and Manon claimed that she had given her baby to a mermaid. Then they carted her away to the asylum, and Jason went back to a house that was so empty and so quiet he left immediately, and found some solace in the rocking and rush of the waves.

They shouldn't have named her Nimue. They shouldn't have named her after the Mermaid, people whispered at the IGA.

In the dawn of springtime, through high spring, Manon would scatter and plant lupine seeds. She did so violently, recklessly, letting the seeds catch where they would on the crags and hills by the water. Lavender and bright purple lupines surrounded Jason and Manon's home like ocean around an island. Her kisses of lupines grew in Mackerel Sky meadows and lined the Paths and blessed Burrbank's Aerie, Maximus soaring high above.

After Nimue's cenotaph was erected, Manon planted lupines around it in the cemetery. Manon would find packages of seeds on her doorstep, gifts of the kind folk of Mackerel Sky.

Manon herself owned only a single lupine in a pot on the porch of her apartment, a great salmon-colored eruption whose seeds she had coveted and planted with precision and care. It came from the first lupine she had ever planted, building a garden with her daughter in front of their house that first summer they shared. She began scattering the seeds to the wind four Augusts later, the summer her daughter went into the sea, as if she could regrow memory. She felt containing the flowers to her own garden was heartless, selfish, and so set them free.

Like my daughter, she thought.

The salmon lupines grew in the wake of the Paths she walked daily, carrying her child, inside and outside of her body. When the lupines bloomed in spring, spears of coral wildfire lined the veins of the Paths that Manon and Nimue and Jason loved, even though as a family they would never walk them again.

Almost every gardener in town grew one of Manon Perle's lupines. They were almost as famous as her quilts of the Nine Tales of Mackerel Sky, elaborate pictorial representations of the Burrbank and Nimuë legend. Some she stitched together when she was a new wife, some she stitched together when she was pregnant, some while her baby slept, and some when she was clinically insane. Into nine quilt panels she sewed the legend of Mackerel Sky's founding, history bubbling out of fabric, panels showing the misfit crew and violent battle with the pirates and the marooned *Bellaforte*, and always in the center was the Kiss, the Mermaid saving the drowning Captain with her breath.

Manon had dreams sometimes where the mermaids came to her in the ocean and split open her womb like a bear trap. They stuck their lithe pearlescent fingers inside her and then ripped her apart. She then turned the night ocean blacker with her blood, and three mako sharks feasted on her flesh.

Such was the violence of her grief.

But on rare occasions, the dream played out differently, and the mermaids would kiss her, and pleasure her with their fingertips, and out of her womb emerged two fishtails, and Manon became a mermaid. She then swam and swam, swam away from everything into the dark with her daughter beside her, and believed everything could be beautiful again.

But most of the time it was the sharks.

Jason couldn't understand what she did, when she cast their child into the sea, why she cast their child into the sea, so he didn't know how to process or forgive her and instead shut down and pushed her away, overtly, subtly, daily, until he was encased safely in distance. He didn't know that he didn't need to drive her away, that she was already adrift on the Atlantic, an exile in her mind, wishing her dead child would quicken in the ocean's womb. Jason could have anchored her had he told her he still loved her, had he told her there was nothing they could do, that she was a good mother, had he held her, but in his grief he couldn't find the words, and his arms lay limply at his sides. He did not reach for her.

Manon spent three stints in the mental hospital near Augusta the year after Nimue died. She took the longest of showers there, willing herself away in water, staring down into the drain. Somedays she'd imagine herself in a painting of the ocean at night, lit by the lantern of moon, surrounded by a net of mermaids the color of quartz, aubergine, green copper, each with a gentle internal glow. Some had one tail that flicked with fins transparent and lined like the chitin of butterfly wings, some had two tails that curled illicitly outward from their core. One swam so deep her eyes were naught but pearls in the dark. The mermaids regarded her attentively, waiting for her to drown of her own accord, the moonlight reflected on their skin even in the dark of the deep.

When Manon returned from the institution, she'd become a waif who eventually drifted out of the house she shared with Jason, leaving him and their life, and haunted an apartment near the Lone Docks where she lit candles in her windows for the dead. She left her job teaching to sew quilts by the water's edge, her quilts that told the local stories and eventually sold to tourists for thousands.

She stitched these quilts with three ancient firecracker women—Gladys, Agathe-Alice, and Beatrix, known as the Three Bats—who had histories upon histories and two husbands between them. Kids whispered they were witches and descendants of the Piratebird, a woman stowaway aboard the *Bellaforte* who eventually became Burrbank's land-bride. There were so many lifetimes of overlapping love triangles among the three Sisters and their men that it's said it caused the one dead husband's stroke. They were called many things: the Sisters, the Wharf Bitties, but the Three Bats stuck most soundly. Manon found comfort in their waxing and waning consciousness, steady hands, and infallible connection to each other.

Manon had known them for years, but one afternoon, when she was walking the Lone Docks, Gladys beckoned her over with a knitting needle.

"You need a place to stay," the old woman said, and all three nodded in their rocking chairs.

Manon agreed; that afternoon she had decided to move out and search for an apartment.

"We have a room. Up there." She pointed with the needle to a door. It opened to a set of steps that led to the upper rooms of their little house with a small deck that overlooked the great blue of the ocean.

Manon moved in that day. She began the nightly ritual of sitting with them on their front deck, stitching her quilts. Most of the time she was silent and listened, comforted by the cadence of their conversation and the clinking of the knitting needles. They knitted and sewed and crocheted. They had gifted Manon with a large crocheted scale-patterned baby blanket when Nimue was born. It became her favorite blanket. It was wrapped around her when she went underwater.

"I saw a mermaid," Manon told them once. "She asked for my dead child."

And when her daughter went down,

    down,

     down,

     Manon went away,

    away,

  away.

The Three Bats nodded, patted her on her arm. Agathe-Alice, the only one in a wheelchair, her legs wrapped in a thick afghan, rolled closer and grabbed her hand.

"That won't happen here."

Manon liked that they never looked at her the way most of the townsfolk did, never whispered when she walked by, "She dropped her baby girl into the ocean. Like a goddamned sacrifice."

The Sixth Square

You must embrace me, land,

says the sea

as the water is coming over the edge

as the water is coming over the edge

the sirens are singing

and their song

has split the seam of the heart of the depths

its core, its truth is signaling

to me, you must embrace me,

as the water is coming over the edge

*D*errick wrote poems of Mackerel Sky and of the Captain and the Mermaid and the Piratebird's love affairs and of the town's curse.

He wrote them from his dead mother's notes and old records in the library and mutterings he heard from the Three Bats who sewed the quilts with mad Mrs. Perle in rocking chairs by the Lone Docks. He wrote them from what he imagined and dreamed mermaids and mermen to be like. He wrote them from the crevasses of the breaks in his heart, from love, from longing.

Derrick liked the Three Bats, a lot. He spent years at the library after his mother's death sitting at their skirts listening to them tell stories of mermaids and their town. They brought him homemade treats every day, snickerdoodles and chocolate crinkles and date bars, a balm of baked goods that some days lessened his grief. They gave him jobs that made him official and important: he was the only one allowed to push Agathe-Alice's wheelchair in the library; he was the only one allowed to gather all the biggest books and give them to Widow Pines to reshelve. Most importantly, in the darkest, wettest days after his beloved mother drowned, in those days when the solid ground eroded underfoot, the spumes pulling the land into the main, and Derrick floundered, his anchors, despair and grief, sinking deep into the dark, the three old ladies made him laugh uproariously. Beatrix often belched suddenly, exuberantly, and without shame, for her hearing aid never worked as it should and thus she was blissfully unaware of how her burps echoed through the cavernous library. Beatrix did see the laugher bubbling out from Derrick in the aftermath, and sat content in the knowledge that she must have said or done something wonderfully funny to make him react so, as there was no better antidote to grief than unbridled, escaped joy. Gladys swore like a cocky pirate and would never lower her voice no matter how many times Widow Pines (or parents or schoolteachers) asked. So every time Gladys visited the library, she would always end up banished to the storehouse room right next to the old waterwheel. Derrick always went to sit there with her for a spell; he liked to watch the waterwheel turn, and before she would calm down and read to him, he got to listen to her inevitable grumpy tirade against the tyranny of Widow Pines and learn lots of new words that no other adult would teach him. Agathe-Alice liked to have him race her around the library in her wheelchair, until Widow Pines, of course, brought down the checkered flag.

"No wonder your husband left you," tossed Agathe-Alice. Here was one of the reasons Derrick loved the Sisters. Sometimes he simply could not believe what they said out loud.

"Drowned, you old bat. There is quite a difference. Race course is closed for the day," Widow Pines volleyed. Her husband had been dead some thirty years.

"Yes, yes, God rest his soul. Pretty sure he is one of the merfolk now. Like me, you know." Agathe-Alice jokingly patted the afghan that was always wrapped around her motionless legs. "I bet he just dove off your boat and swam away."

"He never climbed onto your boat now, did he?" Widow Pines said, silently slipping a hardcover into its stack.

Almost inaudible, the shout—"Fucking right!"—came from Gladys all the way back by the wheelhouse. Derrick didn't understand what they were talking about; he didn't think any of the Three Bats owned boats.

As he got older, he saw them less in the library and more on the baseball field. They came to all of his games and sat at third base, where they knitted in deck chairs and ruthlessly trash-talked the umpires and the other team. They brought the home team cookies wrapped warm and never shared with the opposing side; if anyone tried to sneak a treat, Gladys rapped them on their grubby knuckles with a knitting needle. Derrick always hugged them after every game.

He was happy to hear that the Sisters had taken Mrs. Perle into their sewing circle. He lost his mother. He couldn't imagine Mrs. Perle's grief over losing her little girl. He did anything he could to distract himself from his sadness—this was why he was such a good pitcher, such a voracious reader. He imagined sewing helped old ladies, so sewing quilts must help Mrs. Perle.

And Mrs. Perle's quilts were famous. They depicted the town's legend of Burrbank and the Mermaid in nine squares: the Crew of the *Bellaforte*, the Pirate Attack, Nimuë, the Shipwreck, the Kiss, the First Betrayal, the Second Betrayal, the Third Betrayal/Torch Night, and the Broken Sunrise.

Although she sewed in solitude and en plein air with the old ladies in their rocking chairs, she often sewed them during her students' study hall or creative writing or homeroom. Administration and students let her be, especially because her quilts sold for thousands and she donated money to the school. And everyone knew her baby died and she went crazy.

Every year at Mackerel Sky's annual summer Mermaid Festival, a quilting contest was held, a rooted Down East tradition. One year, Mrs. Perle's entry, "The Moorings of Mackerel Sky," her first quilt depicting the mermaid legend of her hometown, blew the competition away, won first place, and was bought by a movie star for his daughter. From then on, a quilt from Mackerel Sky became a tourist necessity. Manon's quilt ignited an art spark, and when the following year the Mermaid Festival Committee announced that the quilting contest theme would be "The Mermaid Legends of Mackerel Sky," quilters in their houses off the Paths sewed the town's legend in nine quilt squares, following Mrs. Perle's layout, stitching their signatures in mermaid scales and blazing buildings and drowned men. They displayed the finished quilts in the town church; Manon's won first prize again, and every single quilt was purchased by the end of the festival. The next year Mrs. Perle did not enter the quilting contest but donated her quilt to the auction that happened after Beano on the second-to-last night of the Mermaid Festival. It sold for eighteen thousand dollars. People whispered Mrs. Perle had a waiting list a hundred names long.

Derrick couldn't help but be drawn to the mermaids. His mother had always been fascinated by their lore, their connection to their home. He thought he and his dog, Duke, saw a mermaid once, near the salt marshes by the lighthouse, but he couldn't be sure, and Duke wanted nothing to do with it. He wished he had someone he could tell, but he didn't want anyone to think him crazy, or weird, or worse . . . so he told no one, and Duke carried one more secret. He again missed talking to his mother. He had asked her many times if she believed mermaids were real.

"We don't know what we don't know," she always replied serenely, fingers tapping on her favorite leather journal.

Mrs. Perle often used the mermaid tales in her creative writing class. Though many students had heard the stories many ways before, hearthside or graveside, they listened again for what they had not yet heard or for the parts they loved. Some imagined themselves as part of Burrbank's crew, sailors from almost every ocean with strange histories fighting pirates in the dark of night; some loved the moment Burrbank finally laid eyes on Nimuë and fell utterly, fully in rapturous love; some listened for the part when the Piratebird rallied the women of Mackerel Sky to fight off the mermaids, the women setting parts of their beloved homestead ablaze, for mermaids were terrified of fire, and while they listened to the story they imagined themselves brandishing sabers and standing bare breasted, backlit by a world burning around them.

In her creative writing class, Mrs. Perle gave an assignment to write a short story (or set of poems or comic strip) retelling one of the parts of the mermaid legend. Derrick was writing about the First Betrayal, usually portrayed on the sixth square of the quilts, when Burrbank kissed the Piratebird.

Burrbank's true love, the mermaid Nimuë, disappeared into the depths for months and years at a time. Nimuë and the mermaids left an abundance of fish in their absence so that Burrbank's men never went wanting, though all except the Captain were uneasy at accepting the gifts from them.

Burrbank was a clever, observant communicator with a trustworthy reputation, a hard line, and an intimidating parlay bookended by his crew the Terror in the Night and the Tattooed Twins. He befriended the Wabanaki and traded in furs and salt and pearls. Burrbank and the town would later capitalize on lumber, and from this trade formed the skeleton of Mackerel Sky. The gifts from the ocean were the town's wet, new skin.

It all came with a price.

The first betrayal was a kiss.

When they weren't lobstering, the boys of Mackerel Sky went to the beach to look at the Mermaids. The Mermaids were the school mascot, also a townie nickname for the girls. Derrick joined them, but by seventeen he already knew he had fallen in love with Ricky, and Ricky was about as far in the closet as Narnia, so, no hope for love, he went to the beach to go to the beach. Iterations, stories, images of Nimuë and her tribe of mermaids peppered Mackerel Sky like coral and shells on a seashore: the school mascots of the Mermaids and the Tritons, the summer Mermaid Festival, the quilting contest, the boat tours, the touristy shops, the ordinal mermaid sculptures on the green and in the cemetery. During the festival, many pageants were held, including the Miss Mermaid and Miss Mackerel Sky beauty pageants (replete with Jr. Miss, Lil Miss, and Pretty Baby versions).

Women of Mackerel Sky either identified as a Nimuë, the mermaid who Burrbank loved so recklessly, or as an Esmeralda, the Piratebird, who eased his tormented heart.

Mrs. Perle retold the legend to her class. Before the *Bellaforte* marooned off the Maine coast, it was attacked by pirates. They came at night, in oily waters, surrounded by an uneasy fog in the wake of the madness wrought by the mermaids. The mermaids were still dogging the ship, and the fear they brought was as all-encompassing as the fog. The crew was off their guard.

That night, Burrbank woke in his bunk to an unnatural stillness, a collective inhalation, and immediately he knew he needed to be on deck. In backyards, with flat lobster trap sticks as swords and acorns as cannonballs, many packs of Mackerel Sky kids had reenacted the great pirate battle, where swords clanged near the rigging, Burrbank was gutted and wounded, and the boat was set aflame. The crew of the *Bellaforte* fought valiantly and prevailed; Burrbank set the pirates, minus their captain, adrift in a lifeboat and sank their vessel, though not before pilfering their coffers and discovering the Piratebird, a young woman captive in the belly of their ship.

She was bloody and barefoot, belched up with the bilge. The pirate captain had claimed her and kept her in the cell, leaving his crew to salivate like dogs around her cage, whispering slithering and biting sentiments to the lips between her legs. Then the captain would take her to his cabin, and she would bleed. When Burrbank cut her bonds she cut out the pirate captain's tongue and then his throat and fed him to the sharks.

Her name was Esmeralda Alewife, and she was a flame-haired, hot-headed fisherman's daughter who grew up under her father's legs on a boat her whole life. When she came aboard the *Bellaforte* she was nineteen. They called her the Piratebird, because she preferred the rafters of the ship, her hair a fire in the air.

Burrbank once asked her under starlight how she came to be the pirate's captive. She explained she was a stowaway.

"You chose to board that ship? What did you intend, fool bird!"

"That pirate captain murdered my father. I intended to slit his throat and feed him to the sharks. The tongue was improvisation."

He looked at her then, and for a moment in her eyes he saw a map of stars.

He ferried the Piratebird to the mainland. She lingered in Mackerel Sky for a few weeks, then disappeared for a decade.

She returned, sword at the hip and sea-leg steady, her hair licks of honey flame, versed in two native tongues, pretty as an autumn afternoon and smoldering like a harvest fire. Burrbank had been steadily building his tiny empire on the ocean coast, marooned to his mermaid; in ten years Mackerel Sky had become a bustling port town and trade stop. When the Piratebird returned, she made Burrbank remember he was human, that he navigated the oceans and was not anchored to only one shore: that he did what he wanted.

And the mermaid he had loved for this decade had been gone, for the longest stretch yet, nearly a year, and Burrbank was dangerously sure she would never return. He searched for her at High Cliffs, but saw nothing but the billow.

Derrick wrote that when Burrbank kissed the Piratebird for the first time, some sort of weird butterfly effect occurred wherein their entangled breath subtly changed the humidity of the wind, the heavier air moving a mosquito to bite a dog, who yelped and then began barking, which scared a flock of seagulls, who pooped on a crab, who crawled toward the ocean and was eaten by a fish, who was eaten by a bigger fish, who swam near a school of fish, which changed their direction so they swam right as opposed to left around Nimuë, her skin the color of moonlight in the deep water, her pregnant belly stretched taught under full breasts, tiny kicks of her child from Burrbank creating their first ripples in the ocean from the womb.

Somehow, she knew. Somehow, she knew; far, far away,

enveloped by the depths, despite the chaos of her changing body, somehow Nimuë knew that Burrbank had betrayed her.

Within her, next to their growing baby, a spark of anger was kindled.

In her womb the child, in her heart the anger, they grew as twins.

Singing Eccentricities

*D*ecorating the windows of the elementary school were third-grade collages of the parable of the Lion and the Lamb. The lambs were done with way too much glue and cotton balls; yarn created the manes for the lions. The children learned that if at the beginning of March the weather in Mackerel Sky bit at the window frames and the doors and shutters, if it roared like a lion, then sometimes at the end of the month the weather teased more fine, more gentle, like a lamb.

Either way, at the end of that March Myra Kelley turned

her back on winter. She did not do this blindly; she was well aware winter would melt and refreeze for weeks or possibly months yet, but during the sunny days she refused to wear her winter coat and began to thaw her blood, crunching the heavy snow with her boots so it melted faster in the weak sunlight, walking around like she could warm the weather with will.

Today the lambs were basking. It was one of the few lucky days at the end of March where the month itself changed its mind about being winter; it simply shed its coats and skin and scales and walked naked through the streets boldly, briefly, deciding today it was spring, and all marveled at its sweetness. Today, Myra wore no coat.

She thought a lot about the boy, little, skinny, puking Leo, wondered if he even had a winter coat, wondered if he would return, wondered how much skinnier he would be. She worried about what kind of bed he slept in at night and if his house smelled like cat piss and what he ate for dinner. She worried and wondered so much she tripped over one of the stupid chickens. One of the posts of the chicken coop was splintered and broken from the crash, and Myra had tried to wrap more chicken wire around the holes so at least the annoying little cretins were contained and wouldn't wander into the street and get run over. Myra gave her DIY job a nine out of ten, because only one of the chickens managed to escape besides the one that was still missing. Leo would do the real work of mending the coop, she thought as she dropped the hen back in the cage. If, of course, he returned.

Dog barked. He had found the missing chicken. Wounded, it had frozen to death in the snow. Myra cried four tears for it. The first tear escaped; the second she tried to brush away; but the third and fourth she accepted and let come.

Myra was a good griever. She looked death in the face and nodded in mutual respect. At little Nimue Perle's funeral she had walked right up to Manon and wrapped her in a bear hug.

"This is right shit," she'd said.

Myra had buried her whole family and her heart, her husband of fifty-five years, Bernie, in the soil of Mackerel Sky, and had made more ham-salad sandwiches for wakes at church halls for drowned fishermen than she cared to remember. Death was a part of life. But this morning, on the sparkling snow in the pale light of spring, the sounds of drips and lapping water and chickadees, the flowing feathers on the frozen chicken carcass were a blight on the landscape, like a cigarette burn on a bedsheet.

Then Leo came shuffling up the hill, two months early, hands shoved deep in the pockets of his Pats sweatshirt.

"You lost, kid? Or ain't got a calendar?"

Leo shrugged and scuffed. "Just walking."

He saw the dead chicken. "Aw shit, Miss Myra. I'm fu— I'm sorry." The catch in his voice was like a lone church bell.

Myra looked at him then, his hollow, shadowed eyes, grimy sweatshirt, dirt under his fingernails, lingering at her stoop like Dog had done years ago.

She nodded, once. "Today seems as decent a day as any to

fix a chicken coop. Let's eat, then. Come on, Dog is barking his fool head off."

Some kids at the IGA spending allowance money on chips and candy said that Myra Kelley was a witch. No one said crazy; she had too much damn sense. Her witch label was mostly circumstantial: she was old; she lived alone; she had a big scruffy dog and probably secrets and definitely a pantry that sometimes smelled of rotten garbage in the summer.

"But she gives out good candy at Halloween" was usually the solid counterargument.

"There's her book" was always the trump card, the definitive smirk, mic drop, King of the Mountain, definitive proof that old Mrs. Kelley by the duck pond was a witch.

Myra kept a great brocaded book, supposedly an artifact from the *Bellaforte* itself. What was contained within was and had been anyone's and everyone's guess. Some gossiped that it was Captain Burrbank's ledger and perhaps his notes on the founding of Mackerel Sky, while others whispered that it was full of spells and traps for catching mermaids. Everyone knew about it, because one year during the Mermaid Festival a tourist in a suit from the city came with a briefcase and a thick wallet asking around about it at the Mermaid's Tail Tavern.

As good, loyal fisherman do, everyone clammed up, and the suit left empty-handed.

The tome was so famous the townies had a saying about it: "Go put it in Myra Kelley's damn book if it's that important to ya."

It wasn't a great saying, but Mackerel Sky was known for its mermaids, not its orators.

Leo wondered if it was real. Leo wondered if he would get to see it.

Leo liked books, a lot of times they were the healthiest alternative to the life around him.

The boy followed Myra followed by Dog followed by the screech and slam of a screen door through the pantry into the kitchen, and he saw bagged Cheerios and onions and dog food and felt a shift in the air from sharp spring snow to pantry and homestead. The kitchen was small, bookended by a coffee pot and an electric water heater, morning and afternoon rituals, respectively. Myra began taking out crabmeat and mayonnaise and white bread and shooed Leo along to the living room with a glass of lemonade.

The living room was slit with long windows, and all Leo could see was ocean, the ocean on all sides, the surface where water met sky a blur of one evaporating into the other, an impressionist painting. Glass cabinets full of stark seashells collected from over seventy years of walking multitudes of beaches reflected the spring light. The walls were full of books.

On a lone stand sat a thick maroon book, heavy and closed. Leo stepped toward the stand, holding the empty glass of lemonade. Some said that that man in his fancy car and his fancy suit had once offered Mrs. Kelley five thousand dollars for the book, and she had said it wasn't for sale.

"It was ten thousand," Myra said, suddenly behind the boy. "And I swept him off my porch with my broom. It's just a really old scrapbook, of sorts."

She had surprised Leo; he jumped and was happy he had guzzled his lemonade so he had nothing to spill. He pointed to the book.

"So is this it, then? Your book? The book? The one with Burrbank's notes, and drawings of the mermaids? And spells?" Leo had speculated about what spells the book contained, of course, maybe even the Mermaid's curse, the words that she spoke when she cursed the town of Mackerel Sky on Torch Night and all those inhabitants drowned. Variations of this spell had been repeated for generations, mostly drunkenly, many times over graves in the oldest part of the cemetery, and most recently over the mermaid statue on Nimue Perle's cenotaph.

"Spells, huh," Myra responded vaguely. "Eat up, kid."

He followed her into the kitchen and did, three crabmeat sandwiches and two glasses of lemonade, Dog's shaggy head resting on his feet, eyes begging forlornly.

"They say, Miss Myra, that no one can see spells in the book except at certain times. It's magic. Mermaid magic." He nodded, eyes big, punctuation on his points. Kids sometimes said pretend spells, drunk over Mrs. Perle's baby's grave, he wanted to tell Myra that too, but didn't. He didn't think that was appropriate, plus he didn't even want to talk about alcohol, because he was never drinking again.

"Lunar magic," Myra said softly, her voice easing into the cadence of the tides, a storyteller's voice. She pushed her last half of sandwich toward Leo, who grabbed it and ate it mindlessly, harnessed by the subject. "Blood magic. Salt circles, the like. Horseshit." She slammed her fist down on the table and laughed. Leo couldn't tell if she was telling the truth or making fun of him. She didn't clarify. Dog put his big head in Leo's lap, and the warmth and weight was wonderful. Leo petted his head. Dog closed his eyes.

"Dog says it's time to fix the coop."

Leo looked at Dog, who was clearly falling asleep, but Mrs. Kelley had been so nice and made good sandwiches, so to Dog's dismay, Leo stood up, at attention.

"Tools and wood are in the barn. If the coop turns out nice and I don't have to do much, I might just feed you again."

Leo did solid, silent work, Dog dogging his heels. Myra tried to shoo Dog into the house, but neither the boy nor the dog would have it so she let it be. Leo got three solid hours in and stopped for nothing except to chug two glasses of lemonade and eat some banana bread Myra made. The chickens were contained, and Myra was satisfied with the work. She called him back to the house just as the wind was picking up and the fog rolling in.

"Leo boy, come in out of the storm."

Myra had a big wraparound porch hung with singing eccentricities—wind chimes, mobiles, bird feeders, buoys. They were dancing marionettes in the wind.

"Your bird feeders are empty," Leo said, pointing. "You got any birdseed?"

"Have. Do you *have* any birdseed? Yes, in the pantry."

"Birds are hungry. I'll fill it."

"Blue bucket in the pantry. Spill some when you fill the feeders—there's a big ole turkey that pecks around here sometimes. He likes the east corner, under that skinny feeder there. He hasn't been around much lately, since he got caught in the woodchuck trap and got mighty mad." Myra caught a smile and made sandwiches again while Leo filled the feeders.

"What's that?" Leo asked later, his mouth full of sandwich. He was pointing to a piece of furniture, a wooden monstrosity that encroached on passersby in the hallway—a cabinet of sorts, a jumble of chests, bookshelves, drawers, and small doors, fat in the middle and curved upward like a grin, two cabinets with glinting glass like eyes. Some drawers were thin and long and wide, some perfectly square, all with keyholes.

"My Christmas cabinet. Is that your second sandwich? Chew with your mouth closed."

"Third," said Leo with open-mouthed chews. "What's a Christmas cabinet? It looks old."

"Ayuh. My great-grandmother used to store her Christmas decorations in those three drawers there, so growing up we called it the Christmas cabinet. Sometimes names just stick."

Leo understood. He had been branded with the nickname Clipper by kids at school swiftly after his infamous car accident. He took it in stride; he had been dealt fiercer blows. The only thing that bothered him about it was that it reminded him of the chicken and the barn and what he did to Mrs. Myra, and she seemed like a nicer old lady than everybody guessed.

Myra waved him forward, and welcomed him, so Leo began rifling through the Christmas cabinet.

"What do you keep in it?" Some of the drawers and doors in the jigsaw jumble of wood were locked and some weren't, some were empty and some weren't. One chest, a bit bigger than a shoebox, didn't open and looked really old to Leo. He discovered skeleton keys, baubles, folded pages of letters, maps, coins, and a compass.

"Oh, this and that. Things that don't have homes, things I can't find a proper place for. Stories. Histories. Magic. You know, witch stuff." Leo's eyes shot up, and Myra laughed. "That was Bernie and I the morning of our senior beach party." Leo was holding a photograph with scalloped edges of a smiling young couple in bathing suits. She wore high shorts like sailor pants, with buttons up the front, and had dark lips and soft curls, her head tilted toward his chest. He leaned against the boulder behind him, his bare feet crossed, short-sleeved button-down open to the sun, big eyebrows and full smile.

"The Book Burner. That's what we call the senior beach party now. *Holy shit!*"

"Mouth, boy."

"Sorry." He swallowed the rest of his sandwich. "How tall was your husband?" He was gaping at a yellowed newspaper article, a photo of Bernie and his sternman flanking a giant hanging halibut. The fish towered over them.

"Six foot six. That fish was nine feet long."

"Wow," he said reverently. "That's so cool, Miss Myra."

"I'll admit, it was something to see that day on the docks," Myra reflected. She remembered that Bernie's smile that day ignited her blood. "All right, deah, you are all done working for the day."

Leo, who had been busily rummaging through drawers and opening cabinet doors, suddenly stood really still. It looked to Myra as though he might cry. She didn't miss a beat.

"You any hand at cribbage?" Myra asked.

"Dunno how to play."

"Come learn, then."

The gray light of the incoming storm highlighted their hands and the cards as they shuffled and dealt. It illuminated their faces, Leo's brows drawn, biting his lip as he pondered the new rules and his next move. As the light faded, and the rain came and left, Myra's hand stuck the final peg.

"If you want, kid, you can come back tomorrow after school to continue the work."

Leo did want to come back; in fact, he found at the door frame he didn't want to leave the warm light and garlicky smell of the old woman's old kitchen.

Long after Leo said goodbye, Dog whined at the door. Myra called Sheriff Badger and gave him what-for regarding the boy's situation. She then got out of her rocking chair and walked to the Paths directly out her gate. Her stepping stones connected to the great crescent footpath that forked to High and Low Cliffs. Myra headed toward High Cliffs, toward the water, carrying the dead chicken, Dog her shadow, the sunset setting her back aflame.

Born to Die

Like every lost boy's nightmare,
the pirates come at night.
Tears
are the sweetest
warmest
wettest
water
for mermaids to bathe
    —Derrick Stowe

I have heard the mermaids singing, each to each. I do
not think that they will sing to me.
        —T. S. Eliot

*T*he doctors kept speaking. She was hearing them but not comprehending.

. . . *lack of blood flow to lower extremities* . . .

Manon thought about how no one ever truly slept in hospitals. The incessant hums, the blinking, the endless loop of television maze, the nurses taking vitals, never truly dark or quiet enough for sleep. A foundation of numbing white noise; if it were to shut off, its absence would be more readily heard, sharp, like a crack.

. . . *causes fusion of the lower limbs* . . .

Crack. Disquiet and dark.

In the hours and days and months after Nimue's birth, as the baby was monitored and grew in an incubator, Manon bled. She found new dark in the dark that was not dark enough for sleep, in the purgatory of sleeplessness, in the pain of recovery, in the silence after conversations with doctors who shared new words that carried no meaning yet, yet already so much weight.

. . . *feet severely interlocked, no rectum* . . .

Jason sat on the rigid hospital couch shocked, silent, and still.

Jason and Manon conceived Nimue on the dining room table on top of a jigsaw puzzle. It had three missing pieces in the end. Manon told Jason she was pregnant one evening when he was coming in from lobstering, at the Lone Docks.

She stepped out on the wharf in the fog, and it surrounded her like she was the pupil of an eye.

. . . no external genitalia . . .

The doctor had later come to them and told them that their baby was biologically a girl, and they named her Nimue.

. . . always need a catheter . . .

Like trying to catch a shadow, Manon sought sleep, but it escaped her. She became a parasomniac in her own personal ring of the Inferno as exhaustion took her in the hospital room.

But when she laid eyes on that precious face, as feminine and soft as a dewdrop, eyelashes thin as spiderwebs, lips a heart the color of red clay, all the pain faded for one moment. *My little mermaid.* Suddenly her love was so fierce that it expanded outside of her and carried her to the warmest of visions—a sea-sparkling summer day on a blanket with baby Nimue, in their future, outside of the hospital.

We will beat this, Manon prayed. *Nimue will survive. A whole, full life, much longer than the doctors say.*

"Your daughter has sirenomelia, an incredibly rare condition where her legs are fused from the waist down. . . ."

Sirenomelia. A new word that with it brought a new world.

When the doctors informed them that Nimue would likely not live beyond ten, if two, if she survived the next weeks, Manon's body and mind, both brought to the brink, shook, shattered, and then shut down. She vomited and shuddered to the core repeatedly until she seized and lost consciousness.

Then and only then Manon finally slept, her body healing miserably slowly, cell by cell by cell. She dreamed of the mermaids; she dreamed of water; she dreamed of an apple orchard in the rain from a long time ago.

When Jason first kissed Manon it was pouring, a drizzly Sunday afternoon in late September. Manon had dragged Jason apple picking to the closest orchards, owned by Ignatius Stebbins, a McIntosh enthusiast and amateur aviator with a barn full of antique planes and fields of fruit. The sky opened up and they took shelter under the branches and the leaves, and he kissed her, lips tasting of raindrops and apples.

After that, no other kiss would do. Manon tried others, sure, and so did Jason, but only Jason anchored her heart, only Jason carried the cookstove, something her long dead father used to say.

Her dream shifted, and she left the apple orchard, and suddenly she was in her childhood bedroom with her dad.

"Luke's not coming."

Manon had flung herself on the bed, a tumble of eighteen-year-old angst. Her father weathered her waves as well as any good lobsterman could; today he sat on the corner of her bed as the sobs wracked and ricocheted and weakened. When he thought he could get an answer, he asked, "Why won't he come?"

"He doesn't want to drive his new car over the dirt roads of the Barrens to get to our house. Stupid dirt roads. Stupid car." The Barrens were blueberry fields that erupted in an indigo brushfire in August. They had dirt roads that ran like veins through them, but the roads were unpaved and rocky.

Manon's father's teeth set in the back. He pointed out the window across the ocean to Iledest Island. He was not a fan of Luke, the Beals Island boy his daughter had been seeing.

"Do you see that? Do you see the island, girl? The Reach?"

Yes, she saw it. She saw the cool green dark of the pines that reached up from the rocks across the cobalt waves, morning sun reflecting off their crests.

"Yes." A petulant syllable.

Her father smelled of brine.

"A man should be willing to swim that stretch of water with a cookstove strapped to his back to come to see you courting, or he ain't worth his weight in salt."

Manon imagined her current beau, Luke, suffering in the chop with a cookstove weighing him down, and that soothed her, even this glittery, sharp-edged morning.

"He wouldn't do it, Dad."

Silence, a length of time.

"Then he ain't worth dating, kid. And he's dumb as a carp."

Manon told her daughter this story the first time when she was three years old, when Nimue asked why Manon and Daddy got married.

"Mama called Daddy from college and he drove a long time to see her. We watched the sunrise over Mackerel Sky that morning." Manon did not tell her daughter that it was two in the morning when she called Jason, or that she wasn't wearing underwear anymore because they had been ripped off during the rape. She didn't tell her that she sobbed most of the car ride back home as the sun rose and bruises bloomed all over her body. Jason drove, stoic, holding her hand steady like an anchor.

Manon told her medical-miracle daughter many stories, because Nimue spent much of her short life in Manon's arms.

Manon made up stories for her girl about everything, household objects, the gardens, the mermaids. The two had a pirate cache of some silly and some priceless treasures, a hair elastic bracelet, a chocolate coin, a skeleton key, beads and baubles, some treasures from their crow friends that lived in the trees behind their house. They also had amassed a small collection of figurines, including an owl landing on a grimoire. Its wings had broken off, one and then the other.

"Talk me a story about it, Momma."

Nimue always fit perfectly nestled in the crook of Manon's right arm, her dominant hand, and carrying hip.

That side ached the most in the late-night lonely dark.

"The wizard's owl has lost his wings. He's reading the magic book to get them back."

Deep intake of breath from little Nimue.

"What if he never gets them back, Momma? What if this?"

What if this. Manon found Nimue's oft-mixed-up words too endearing to correct.

"What if this? Well, then the wizard helps him. But whatever happens, he is a very loved owl."

Manon and Jason let Nimue get her ears pierced a month before her third birthday, because Nimue asked for big-girl earrings, and when you are in and out of hospitals, when you take a complex cocktail of steroids and antibiotics and drugs every day, when your life is to pass as a flash flame, when you are a baby born to die, big-girl stuff happens as early as it can. Perhaps it was a direct retaliation against her life expectancy prognosis, perhaps it was an acceptance of it.

On Nimue's third birthday, Myra Kelley bequeathed the girl a set of antique green pearl earrings so stunning that Manon didn't feel right accepting the gift, but Myra laughed it off and insisted, saying they were just gathering dust in her Christmas cabinet. Manon sterilized the baubles of art, and Myra sat baby Nimue on her lap and put the earrings in.

"Big girls can wear big earrings," she said, and Nimue nodded like it was a commandment.

Nimue wore them from that day on. Manon won a pivotal nighttime battle because she refused to allow little Nimue to wear the jewels to bed, so they compromised by putting them into a leather pouch that Nimue used as a pacifier; she fell asleep each night holding it in her hand. At three and a half she lost the right earring and was devastated, but she continued to wear the other single pearl earring, switching out the left earring with unicorns or mermaids or topaz.

Nimue's nursery was decorated like it was underwater, and in it lived the girl's betta fish in a big bowl. Jason insisted that

Nimue get to name it, so the fish had gone through a myriad of names from Eeee to Bubba to Dada as Nimue's sounds progressed from gurgles to single consonants to words. When Nimue was fully two and understood that things had names, and people named things, the fish went through another revolution of names: Frank, Milo, Leo, Flynn, Christophe, Elsa, ElsaElsa. The betta often looked like it might die. Its spine was twisted, crooked upward like a hook; it swapped swimming for floating around and resting on the bottom of the bowl. Manon and Jason were sure that the betta would be dead by morning, each morning, every morning. So many visitors had asked if the fish was still alive that it became an ongoing joke.

"How's the fish?" Jason would ask Manon.

"Not dead yet." Manon would respond. And they would laugh together at their own stupidity and luck.

Even Nimue would say: "Mommy's fine, I'm fine, kitty's fine, and the fish still isn't dead. So it's good."

The broken-backed betta ElsaElsa lived three weeks longer than little Nimue Perle.

When Nimue died, Manon shipwrecked like Burrbank's great *Bellaforte* during the hurricane of the autumn of 1721—her masts splintered and buckled; her soaked sails lashed and whipped, her deck lolled and splintered in the ombre indigo night. Her hull, her rib cage, was cracked open by the beastly swells and lightning strike. The corpses of her crew littered the ocean. The sails ripped up and disappeared into the sky.

She took on so much water that she was what she was and what she wasn't all at once—a boat that could not float, a ship that could not sail, a mother without her child.

The Christmas Pigs
of Beacon Street

*B*eacon Street slit through the center of Mackerel Sky from outskirts to beach, on clear days, a straight view to the lighthouse. During the holidays it was the most deco- rated street in town; folks competed in categories like "Most Colorful," "Most Religious," and "Miscellaneous." During the Mermaid Festival in August, the parade marched down Beacon Street, a vibrant ribbon of antique cars, truck bed bands, clowns and cops and robbers and beauty queens waving out of sunroofs.

Beacon Street, the spear that intersected the crescent of the cliffs, ran the length of the wealth gamut of Mackerel Sky, from inheritances to food stamps, closets full of clothes with tags still on to patches and hand-me-downs. The farther from the water a Beacon Street resident lived, the less money they had.

The Townsends lived in a ramshackle square one-story house close to the end of Beacon Street, almost to the trailer park turn. The insides of their abode spilled out into every corner of their yard like eviscerated guts—trash bags, plastic toys fading in the sun, shells of cars, beer cans, and cigarette butts. A patchwork fence surrounded the place, a fierce defense built with various materials—chain link, leaning wood, picket, two bait signs, and even an old hull of a boat merged together as strange allies to protect the property. But the fence was moot; the Townsend place was defended by its own energy of disgust, squalor, and a general nastiness that no one wanted to go near.

Save for a few, the Townsends were a pigheaded and big-headed lot. They all complained their family had been cursed, way back on Torch Night—cursed with money troubles and bad luck, brought down low by the government and liberals and the Man—and all believed themselves smarter than the first yet beholden to the last. That itself was the real, true curse: they all believed they were immune to their collective inherited obstinance, that they were not part of their own problem; thus they could never get out of their own way.

Roy and Amber Townsend had three boys, twins Colby and Jared, who were both stocky, selfish, and stupid, and Ricky, the youngest, who was skinny, skittish, and soulful. He came into the world with wide eyes. He was a terrible accident, as both parents liked to tell him, born three years after his brothers, and he liked things that no one in his family could understand: books, violin music, cleanliness, kindness, men. At five he loved a Black baby doll he found discarded on the trailer park road, and his father called him a fag and broke his arm twisting the doll out of it. His mother would have said something, but she lost her voice note by note and word by word a long time ago due to her father, her boyfriends, her husband, and a lifetime of loud, abusive, alcoholic men drowning it out.

Roy heartily accepted that he was a drinker but would punch you wholeheartedly in your smart mouth if you called him an alcoholic. (Just ask his sons, just ask his good-for-nothing wife, Amber, just ask this one bartender in the Ellsworth area.) According to him, two thirty-packs of beer a weekend were, honestly, completely acceptable in all lobstering social circles, especially considering it was light beer. He had set rules for himself, a long time ago: he didn't drink in the morning, he didn't drink coffee brandy or vodka unless it was offered, he didn't spend his paycheck on booze.

When he broke all these rules, a long time ago, he made up

more rules, more exceptions. Alcohol was not affecting his job, the DUIs he had gotten were because of extra summer patrol because of tourists; he switched back to hard liquor because it added less weight around his middle. If he got angry when he was drinking, well, everyone knew better than to piss him off drunk. And nothing he did while wasted counted anyway, because he was on the lash.

Roy was on an elevator down indefinitely, passing many levels of rock bottom—the first time he threw up in public, the first time he pissed himself, the first time he berated his wife and smashed plates in the kitchen, the first time he beat the twins.

Because of the stupid mermaid curse, because of the Man, and because, fuck you, this was a free country, Roy had long given up his drinking rules, and long given up that he had the ability to push buttons on the elevator. Drink would kill him, and he would die willingly splayed on the rock-bottom floor. His family had been cursed that legendary Torch Night anyway, so he might as well go down in style.

One Christmas Roy Townsend inadvertently started the Beacon Street tradition of the Christmas Pigs. He put a lit-up pig in a Santa suit at the apex of his roof. The pig stayed up and mostly lit until Easter, when Roy cut the power to save some money. The pig never got taken down, and the next Christmas one of the richer ladies on Beacon, Thelma Davis, a retired schoolteacher married to a retired doctor, found a collection of Christmas farm animals in a kitsch store in Bar

Harbor, and, thinking the pig so adorable she had to have him, put the pink cutie in the bay window of her big Victorian closer to the coast.

The Mackerel Sky Community Committee awarded her a prize for her decorations that year: she won for "Miscellaneous," twenty-five dollars in an envelope, which she misplaced in her Christmas decorations.

Neighborhood light displays in small towns could be brutally competitive, especially on one of the most prominent roads. The next year, Roy, Thelma, and four other homes on the main drag of Beacon Street included Christmas Pigs in their holiday decorations. (Roy's never left his roof and didn't light anymore on account of being left out all year.) One Christmas Pig was even featured in a manger.

But Roy never won. That could have been the mermaid curse.

Roy's father had complained it was the damn sea skanks that cursed them, but he was a worse drunken shit father than Roy, so Roy never believed him. Roy blamed the Man, the Man with the money that he didn't have.

"I've made my mark on this piece-of-shit town, boys," he said to Colby and Jared, sitting with them and spitting tobacco into a shared empty soda bottle. "Maybe you two will too."

Then he looked at his son Ricky, who was reading a book with his ankles crossed, and spit the tobacco in his general direction.

Ricky hated the Christmas Pigs; they were staunch little

representations of his father's loathing, lit up and mocking and cutesy. Ricky never wanted to hate his father, in the same way he never wanted to grow up poor and unloved. But that was just the hand he was dealt, same as being a fag.

The youngest Townsend always knew he was different from his older twin brothers, but he didn't understand how different until his books and Beat poetry and music drew his nebulous feeling of being an outsider into a term—homosexual—like focusing sunlight through a magnifying glass. Even then, being gay was just a theory, a secret truth that he kept in his thoughts alone, not a reality so therefore not a problem. *I'm just an odd duck, I'm not gay; well, I could be gay, but I've never liked anyone that way; okay, maybe I like someone that way, but nothing is ever going to happen. My dad will kill me. My brothers will kill me.*

But Derrick Stowe, the lanky, sweet brown-eyed boy whose smile stretched the bases, whose baseball jersey never stayed tucked in and lifted up just so when he was slicing the bat through the air for his practice swings, with skin the color of coffee with cream, who kept looking at Ricky in a way that made Ricky feel like cheering for a bases-loaded home run, Derrick made Ricky understand his homosexuality as rock-hard truth. And one night in December, exactly three months before Leo stole the car, when Ricky embraced Derrick for the first time, he embraced himself.

The sense of community in Mackerel Sky, spearheaded by the MSCC, was a tour de force, a creative, aware network of concerned citizens that created life and action when and where there was none. No movie theater? Hold open-air viewings of family-friendly films during the summer months. No ice cream shop? Hold an ice cream social. No real tourism spots except for Burrbank's outcropping on High Cliffs and Nimuë's flat rock off of Crescent Beach? Create the Mermaid Festival, a three-day celebration of Mackerel Sky's relationship to the sea sirens and of small-town living.

Every December the MSCC held a teen dance, a Christmas formal event for all students in Mackerel Sky (aged thirteen to graduation), their dates, teachers, and chaperones. The church common room was booked, draped in gauze and garland, red bows and fairy lights, and students would drink punch and dance with space for Jesus until "Stairway to Heaven" played. The Three Bats were always chaperones; they attended every dance wearing breathtaking tiaras and sat knitting or quilting and critiquing the dresses.

The night of the December dance was cold, but not frigid, and a light snow fell, enough to make things pretty but not precarious. After and during the dance the juniors and seniors snuck out to their pickups for long pulls off stolen liquor bottles and shared cigarettes. Derrick was drinking with his baseball buds, and all three Townsend boys pulled up to share a pint. Ricky ended up leaning next to Derrick on the bed of the pickup, laughing, warm from the liquor, warm from the closeness of the Tritons' pitcher. Their hands accidentally touched behind their backs, and neither moved, each feeling the other's pulse. Then their fingers laced, and something else, unspoken, deeper, heartfelt, laced between them.

That time, no one noticed.

Later that night Derrick and Ricky left the dance and went for a drive. They didn't care where they were going; destinations weren't their destination, proximity was. The roads were slick so they drove slow, music turned low, the bass the only sound. They ended up driving down Beacon Street, the black ocean rippling on the horizon. Ricky told Derrick about the Christmas Pigs.

"I fucking hate them," he said matter-of-factly, and the words felt good and bold.

"Why's that?" Derrick offered, brows incredulous, an indulgent smirk. Ricky liked how he smiled at him, in his grin there was something wicked and exciting.

"They remind me of my dad. My dad hates me, for lots of reasons." Ricky didn't elaborate, but Derrick could infer one major reason, so he nodded sagely without speaking, and their bond intensified. Derrick's father was a rigid, traditional, stoic sort of man, but he wasn't a bigoted asshole drunk like the Townsend patriarch. Stéphane was ultimately kind, and yet Derrick himself had seriously considered remaining in the closet permanently, and entering into a loveless marriage with some dull townie just to avoid talking to his father about the subject at all, so he couldn't imagine what Ricky was facing. Ricky's father was a piece of work. Roy Townsend had been pulled off more than one drinking buddy and escorted home on more than one occasion. He had a permanent ban at the Mermaid's Tail. Derrick understood completely why Ricky hadn't come out. His father would beat the shit out of him. So Derrick did what he wished someone would do for him when he was floundering in the middle of the violent confluence of identity and sexuality and self-confidence. He reached out, and offered a bit of his own vulnerability.

"I write poetry," Derrick replied.

He didn't yet say *I'm gay*, but he thought that poetry was close enough code-speak.

"I come from a family of fishermen, and I can't swim." *I'm gay too*, revealed Ricky in the same speak. And then a sentence that made Derrick's lonely heart swell: "I'd like to hear some of your poetry sometime."

They rode in silence for a bit, the snow falling in time to the bass notes, the moment perfectly preserved like an inhalation, like a shaken snow globe, all the flakes momentarily swirling.

Beacon Street curved open wide to Crescent Beach, at the left tip of the beach, Burrbank's Aerie, where stood the remnants of Burrbank's first house, a foundation and a burned-out hearth, with two mermaid flagstones. The wraparound porches followed Beacon Street's curve. Thelma Davis's husband, complaining the whole time, had strung four Christmas Pigs, a developing sleigh-and-reindeer theme along her wraparound porch.

Derrick couldn't explain why he did it (most likely a combination of recklessness, connection, and peacocking) but he pulled over the car and hopped out, Ricky left with a wide-eyed "what" on his face. Derrick grabbed the closest Christmas Pig from Thelma's porch, pulled it off the railing, and threw the prancing piggy like a pigskin. Shot with Derrick's pitcher's cannon the Christmas Pig arced over the beach and landed face-first, curlicue to the sky, the snout buried in the beach sand. The snowstorm would later cover this up, and Christmas Piggy Number Four would never return to Thelma's porch but instead be found in the spring by some thrilled kids with buckets and shovels.

Ricky got out of the passenger side and kissed Derrick full on the lips, and their first kiss was everything a first kiss should be—beautiful and awkward and full to the brim with hope and promise—and no one saw it this time.

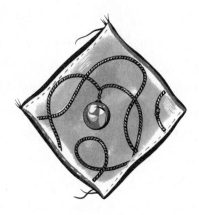

The Seventh-Square Portrayal
of the Second Betrayal

A criss, a cross
Blue thread, storm-tossed
Candles twitch, handkerchief
A mother's stitch
A cut, snap snip
Nacreous moon, listing ship
Palm song sewn, set in quilt
—Song of the Three Bats

*N*imue was in the incubator, so Manon could not breastfeed, and it broke her heart, feeling her breasts fill and then expel the colostrum in agony, none of it going to her baby. Manon remembered thinking that everything was dripping, everything was bleeding, that the body truly was made mostly of water, and it was all coming out. Her nipples leaked milk; she was bleeding into her bandage gauze; she cried and cried. She sat a long, long time on the bath stool in the shower once, methodically squeezing the blood out of a maxi pad. When it filled with water and was heavy, she squeezed. The blood ran in rivulets down her legs. It filled again. Women never stopped bleeding, never, thought Manon.

According to the doctors, sirenomelia was always fatal. The legs could not be separated because the blood vessels crossed side to side. The organs were rearranged, misshapen, the wrong size. They wouldn't last. Nimue had a kidney transplant in Boston at two and was on dialysis. She had two bags, one for urine, one for feces.

At home, Manon carried her daughter everywhere. When Nimue was slightly older, a favorite pastime of theirs was throwing seeds for crows off the back and front porches. Birdseed and bread crumbs and goldfish and cereal, the former Manon's offerings and the latter Nimue's. They did this so long and so often the crows eventually brought gifts back—pretty sea glass and mica and shells. Nimue lined her presents up by size in her room—dimes, acorn caps, a broken necklace clasp.

After Nimue died, Manon fed the crows less and less, the mother a black hole silhouetted against the violent apricot sky. The crows however continued to bring her gifts, every day, long after she forgot to feed them, long after she moved out, long, long after.

One morning they brought her a tiny green pearl earring.

Manon didn't speak much when she returned to teaching almost four years after her infamous Mermaid Festival boat ride, where she went out in the boat with her daughter and returned home without her. She'd give the assignments and walk around, then sit at her desk and sew quilts or stare out the window. Her comments on the stories and poems were sometimes loopy and erratic, if she gave any at all. Mostly she just scratched a check in the corner to indicate the assignment was received and completed, no grades, no words. Everyone agreed she should have stayed away from work for a little longer, but no one could agree on what she should do instead.

"Boys, shut the fuck up," she said to the Townsend twins one day while sipping her coffee, and the entire class went silent for an entire minute before they snickered en masse; it was well deserved.

She drank her coffee out of a mug covered in skeletons. The Christmas when Nimue was one, Jason gave Manon a coffee mug with pictures of dinosaurs. When filled with hot coffee, the dinosaurs' skins faded away to the bones. The mug was never to be put in the dishwasher, but when it inevitably made it in, the dinosaurs—which were nothing but a thin film—crumpled up and disintegrated as they were boiled by the water. It happened in stages, because once the mug was accidentally in the dishwasher it was washed so from then on.

"What happened to the dinosaurs?" Jason asked one day.

"They went extinct," Manon replied.

When she was pregnant, Manon sewed on her quilts every night. The first quilt she sewed was Nimue's crib blanket. She sewed a panel from each of her favorite children's stories, so her daughter's crib blanket was a celebration of hungry caterpillars and little princes and hedgehogs in aprons. When she was pregnant with Nimue she also sewed "The Moorings of Mackerel Sky," her first quilt depicting the mermaid legends of Mackerel Sky with the nine squares. Her rendition of the Kiss, where Nimuë embraced Burrbank underwater like he was her man in the moon, the central square, was her particular favorite. The seventh square's portrayal of the Second Betrayal was toned down to just a net and hook and necklace, because as this was her first quilt, Manon was unsure how to best portray the drowning of the mermaid Nimuë's brother.

The mermaids, as Manon was told it, and as she told it in class, were betrayed a second time by Burrbank and the humans. The First Betrayal was Captain Burrbank and Esmeralda's kiss when Nimuë was pregnant with the Captain's baby. However, the Second Betrayal was more terrible and violent, its consequences were more severe. One of Nimuë's brothers was ensnared by a fisherman's nets—supposedly the Terror's, whose knots were inescapable. Growing tighter during the struggle, like the body of a python, the nets strangled the merman to death, and his necklace, containing a giant verdant pearl, a treasure coveted by the sea folk, was stolen and taken on land. Manon did not want to sew that violent death onto a baby blanket, so she left the merman out entirely but kept his necklace. She used the loveliest piece of sea glass as the pendant, sewing it on securely so that Nimue could never pull it off and choke on it.

Manon sewed whenever she was nervous about being a mother. She wanted to be a good one. The stitches helped soothe her; she could watch the stitches line up and somehow that meant everything would be okay. She stitched before and after that day on the water on Jason's lobster boat, the day her daughter died and sank into the ocean.

Over the months, the quilts replicated themselves, one into the other, nine panels showing the mermaid tale of how Mackerel Sky was founded. In Manon's dreams all she saw were mermaids; mermaids writhing in the water calling to her; mermaids singing their songs and beckoning. Down down down. So she sewed her quilts like her sails and raised them to the wind to keep from sinking.

Her quilts kept her warm on days she bathed herself in the snow and cold and rain.

Jason was a good husband, but at times he could be cold and hard. He didn't know it, but after Nimue died Manon simply needed his hands, for she was held together like a spiderweb on grass. Had he just held her he would have held her together.

When she walked away from their marriage that April, in her head Jason was right behind her. In her head, he was calling her back. In her head, she had already turned around.

When she got into the car and drove away from their marriage, all those thoughts remained. Although it was April, there was still a foot of snow on the ground. She looked out at the winter and thought that such winters were the death and end of settlements.

When Nimue was alive, Manon also stitched children's quilts based on stories. There were Maine stories, the story of Miss Rumphius, who scattered the lupine seeds and painted the Maine coast the colors of berry and lavender and olive, and the story of Sal she quilted in blueberry blue and sand, with berries and bears. But she always returned to quilting the story of Mackerel Sky and the moorings of men and mermaids over and over.

She stitched the lush body of Nimuë the Mermaid on the third square and thought of the legend of Captain Burrbank's arrival on the beach. Manon always used the deepest greens and reflective blues for Nimuë's hair, the colors of the core of the ocean, and she always depicted her with parts hidden, like the striptease of a burlesque dancer.

When Ichabod Burrbank landed to explore, he always sought the highest vantage point on the coast so he could survey the land and sea. Under the full moon, a giant heavy egg ready to crack, he came upon the cliffs. The air was clear and black with pinpricks of white starlight, but Burrbank was anxious, twitchy.

After dogging his ship for weeks, and saving him from the

pirates, the Mermaid had been dogging his dreams still, her prow just on the edge of the gray foggy sea, just on the edge of his vision. She had sent two men from his crew into the sea. One more lost his mind. She made the crew nervous. But Burrbank could not stop thinking about her, about how she kissed him, how she tasted like wanderlust and the secrets of the deep.

As he surveyed the territory from what would become High Cliffs, a bald eagle stretched its wings perched on a magnanimous pine. Burrbank looked down to the beach below.

There, lounging on a rock, the moon illuminating her skin, her eyes shining like opals, the water rushing off her body, begging his hands and mouth to follow, was the Mermaid.

He wanted her like he had never wanted anything before, desperately, madly.

She smiled, vulpine.

And by the time he had climbed down the cliffs and made it to what would be known as Nimuë's Perch, she had disappeared into the sea.

He built a lean-to on the Aerie and slept there that night, waking up every hour to search.

That lean-to become the town of Mackerel Sky.

Besides Burrbank's cenotaph, the most decorated stone in Evergreen Cemetery was the cenotaph of little "Mermaid of Mackerel Sky" Nimue Perle. The flowers planted grew as large as the flowers delivered, Manon's famous salmon lupines at either end. Nimue Perle had become part of local lore, had been on many regional television programs and on the national news twice. She was visited often, posthumously hosting parties, especially during the summer Mermaid Festival and the Day of the Dead. High school students and romantics kissed the little mermaid statue on the cenotaph for luck, especially against drowning and mad love.

Her cenotaph was kept clean and well-tended and somewhat close to Millicent Stowe's grave. Derrick walked by it every Sunday on the way to visit his mother.

Manon did not visit the grave much, for she knew her daughter was still in the sea.

After the third visit to the sanatorium, Manon moved into an apartment on one of the Lone Docks. She couldn't live anymore with Jason; he still blamed her. He didn't understand. No one could understand. Manon knew she would never understand, so how could anyone else? How could anyone comprehend sitting on the back of a lobster boat cradling a dead daughter, and then giving her to a mermaid?

The day Nimue died, Manon sat good and long in Sheriff Badger's car, in the passenger seat, door open, staring at the water through red-rimmed eyes—for hours, or for minutes, time was irrelevant. Desperation and despair played "Ring Around the Rosie" in her head, and a sick emptiness grew in her stomach.

This isn't happening. This isn't happening. It can't be, she kept thinking as her brain began pulling away from the horrifying, devastating reality that now existed for her.

A new thought came in, vicious, violent, galloping through the ballroom of her mind like one of the horses of the apocalypse.

You
bet
your
life
it
is

Bones and Blood from Grief

*M*yra to Manon, on grief:

"You go make a cup of tea. You see that the water boils. You see you can still boil water. You wait. At first, the water is too hot to drink. You wait again. For a moment, just a few sips—just a moment, the swiftest of time—the tea is hot but not scalding, sweet but not sugary, lemony, but not bitter. It is perfect for a moment, so you sip your perfect tea for a moment and look out your window at the waves and see that everything is still moving, but you are perfectly still.

"It's just a tiny accomplishment, a small thing. You realize, even as your body tries to turn itself inside out to bones and blood from grief, you realize you are still capable of making a good, strong cup of tea, that time passes, that the water cools. That life goes on. It will never be the same, but it still can *be*."

A few years after Nimue's funeral, when few people invited Manon Perle around anymore, Myra invited her over one afternoon for a chin-wag and a cup of tea. An afternoon became afternoons. One day, her wedding anniversary, a day of significance to Myra that no one remembered anymore because most of them were dead, Myra spoke to Manon, through tears, staring at the ocean.

"The tea will be good and strong even when you are not. It will steady your hands when the grief comes, and it can be your touchstone when you have a hard cry. The hard cries are good—that's the love we had yet to give them seeking them out. When in doubt, make a cup of tea."

Something clicked in Manon that day; a gear turned, a thought pattern reset, and that night she had a juddering hard cry that came from the bottom of her spine. Then she cleaned her kitchen and saw a clean sink for the first time in months.

Myra Kelley's husband, Bernard Robert Kelley, died the night of their fifty-fifth wedding anniversary, two days after the doctors advised Myra she should gather the family.

He was on life support, but Myra saw no life there; that

gray body breathing through machines was not her Bernie anymore.

Their wedding ceremony ended at 6:24 p.m., and so began fifty-five years of marriage, fifty-five years of a true, working love. So in the hospital at 6:24 p.m. Myra wished Bernie a happy anniversary, and told him she loved him, and kissed his forehead, once again, once more. It was still warm and smelled like him. She tried to give him a final round of hell about leaving her with the chickens, but her laugh shattered into a gut-dragging sob that shook her whole body, as her earth as she knew it split and crumbled and cracked and fell into the sea.

Then she nodded and breathed because she was still breathing.

When it was over, when the steady heartbeat flatlined, and the silence and loss were paralyzing, Myra found again that she had hands, and that the right one was dominant, so she moved it. The air was thick as water, and she could swear she felt everything in the air—every molecule, every current—as she reached out to his eyelids. When she closed his eyes it was with the most profound gentleness, as if she were wiping away tears or releasing a wet-winged monarch. She buried him in his best suit but kept his favorite house shirt hung up in her closet. Myra Kelley wouldn't tell you about it, but there was more than one occasion where she clung to that flannel, sobbing in the closet.

"What was in this, Miss Myra?"

Myra had allowed Leo to rifle through the Christmas cabinet again, as long as he was careful. The rule was that he could open anything unlocked. He liked this rule at first; he knew which drawers he wanted to try next. But the Christmas cabinet proved frustrating; he found that different doors and drawers were locked and unlocked at different times. Right now he was looking at an empty, ancient velvet pouch.

"A necklace with a green stone. It looked like the ocean. I gave it to Millie Stowe's boy right after she died. She was an interesting woman, that Millie. Knew a lot about mermaids."

"What do you mean, Miss Myra?"

She didn't respond.

"What are all these?" Leo pulled open one of the thin, wide drawers of the Christmas cabinet.

"That's a lot of maps, kid. Maps of the stars, maps of Mackerel Sky."

"1679? 1711? Holy shit these are old. Where did you get all this stuff?"

"Ayuh, older than me. Watch your mouth. I inherited it. They came with the Christmas cabinet."

"So you *are* related to Burrbank!"

"Ayuh."

She then told Leo the story of how once Burrbank built his house on the Aerie, he brought his effects from the *Bellaforte*, six months before it was ultimately wrecked and sunk on its mooring by the great hurricane. Burrbank's lockbox, an old coffer with intricate ironwork and a huge lock, sat as the middle base of Myra's Christmas cabinet. The rest of the cabinet built up around the strongbox over generations. The safe was always locked; Leo had tried to open it multiple times. They say Esmeralda, the Piratebird, saved the coffer and what she could stuff into it from the fire that burned down his house.

"But I thought the Piratebird started the fire?" Leo asked.

"Some of them she did because the mermaids were coming for the town. Mermaids are terrified of fire."

Leo didn't understand and pulled out another map, this one of the Paths. He had walked these paths many times by himself, mostly alone and in the dark, but more recently he had walked them at sunset with Myra and Dog.

"You'll find an earlier version of that map in the red book."

"They say that Burrbank started some of the Paths himself, to get the best vantage points of the island."

"That sounds about right—white men taking credit for something they didn't do. No, boy. Burrbank only followed what was already there. The Wabanaki had created the Paths many, many years before."

Energized, the boy turned his attention elsewhere and the pair walked toward the book stand. "Miss Myra, is your red book Mr. Burrbank's book? His actual book?" Leo tried to lift the cover, but the red tome was closed fast. "It won't open."

"He owned it once, yes, but the Piratebird inherited it. And sometimes the book won't open."

Mouth full of sandwich: "Why?"

She didn't respond. Dog began barking to someone coming up over the hill. Leo's stomach dropped. He hoped it wasn't his mother.

But it was Jason Perle, who called out a hello and scratched Dog under the ears. Jason had known Mrs. Myra since he was in diapers, and some of his first work had been yard and boat work for the Kelleys when he was younger than Leo. Right after Jason's brother drowned, Bernie Kelley and his sternman Oswald always seemed to be at the boatyard exactly when Jason arrived and always stayed puttering around their boats and truck beds until after he left, so the first few years that Jason was a lobster boat captain they were always there to help him with boat issues and get him in and out of the water. Then, when Manon and Jason moved in under the hill and they became neighbors, Mrs. Myra helped with the house and then the baby, and Jason helped Bernie do work around the Kelleys' house, especially as Bernie got older, and even more so when he got sicker. Jason visited Mrs. Myra a couple times a week, and silently did odd jobs that he saw needed doing. She always fed him, and since Jason struggled working a microwave, he was immensely grateful.

After visiting with Mrs. Myra for a bit, Jason grabbed his tools and joined a thrilled Leo. They worked together on the barn, Dog winding his way between them. Leo had never been this close to a man before without worrying about being hit.

He liked the way Jason talked to him, gently, smartly, like Leo was a grown-up, like Leo wasn't useless, like Leo had important things to say.

Sheriff Badger rode by that afternoon. He left his car parked on the side of the road and spat out sunflower-seed shells on the walk up to Myra's front porch. Myra was knitting in her rocker watching the boy and Jason work.

The sheriff stood on the stoop and took in the ocean in silence. Myra had known the sheriff all his life, from plastic badges to metal badges, pop guns to rifles. His family was here long before Burrbank, stamping the footpaths into the ground.

"What you knitting there?"

"Hat."

"Ayuh. Looks good. I love mine. Boy giving you trouble?"

"Not so far, but it's early yet."

"Ayuh."

They paused, the sounds of knitting needles between them.

"Do you remember that time in high school Stevie and I got drunk and stole Bernie's father's skiff?" Sheriff Badger asked Myra, chuckling at his own stupidity.

"Ayuh."

"We stove her up good on those rocks, didn't we? Giant hole in the bottom, bent hull. He was some pissed. Our parents happily marched us out the door when he showed up at both our houses at four the next morning and made us start building him a new one. Hungover as all hell."

Myra laughed.

"Sure was nice of him not to bring the police in."

"Yessah. But you owned up and faced up to what you did, and that was really important to his father, and my Bernie."

"All right, then. You let me know if the boy gives you any kind of trouble."

"Will do. You take care, Sheriff. And hug that baby boy of yours."

"Yes, ma'am."

Myra walked to the boy and Jason. "Looks good, boys. You two ready for supper?"

"That would be mighty kind of you, Mrs. Myra." Jason wasn't skinny like Leo was, but Myra knew he did better when he had a woman cooking for him.

"Come on in, then."

Afterward, when Jason went back down under the hill, Leo asked to read the red book again.

"Not tonight. Red book's closed today."

"That's a tragedy."

"Life's just one fucking tragedy after another," said Myra Kelley.

"Whoa! Watch your mouth!"

She smirked and then laughed loudly. "Just because the red book isn't open doesn't mean you can't read. I have book-shelves, Leo boy. Peruse." When he didn't move, she clarified. "It means *look around*."

Leo began to read books each night. She taught him what

some of the words meant and cooked him her husband's old favorite meals and tapped him with her knitting needles when he bit his fingernails. Myra's wooden recipe box, which Bernie had fashioned for her stacks of index card recipes, was always open, dusted with forgotten flour.

"It's brightening up," Myra would state in the morning as the sun was about to break through the fog. Leo then took his tools and got to work. Jason joined sometimes when he came back from the boat. Myra puttered around, Dog and the cursed chickens investigating Myra in the gardens or the boys at the barn.

When spring started blooming into summer, Leo and Myra took breaks on her porch like stretching cats. Myra read trash romance novels and fell asleep with honeybees for company. Leo talked and talked about things Myra knew nothing about—video games and memes and social media. Myra just listened to the boy who had never been listened to before, and chewed on her empty pipe, smiling.

When he slept in the spare room she covered him with the blanket so he stayed warm, and watched until the tension in his shoulders and his furrowed brow relaxed away, and he became a child again, deep in his dreams. The only bruises on Leo's body were those that he had earned being a boy, playing outside with a dog who no longer slept in Myra's bed but snored contentedly in his now-established spot at Leo's feet.

This Ship Is Haunted

Once Mrs. Perle asked Derrick and the students of her creative writing class to describe what true love was like.

Derrick wrote:

> *This ship is haunted*
> *Tip to tine, bow to stern*
> *We would merge like water into earth*
> *Nimuë whispered to Burrbank*

And then Derrick added:

> *His breath has the sweetness of lake morning*
> *he calls me coffee bean*
> *His hands are sandy and sweaty and strong*
> *this whole beautiful day is like déjà vu*
> *so I lie and I lie*
> *under you*

The final attempt in his notebook was:

> *the heart's landscape*
> *dismantled*
> *irrevocably*
> *by his earthquake*

He never said it was good poetry.

Derrick's father, Stéphane, was a distant descendant of the Terror in the Night, Burrbank's Congolese first mate and stalwart friend. The largest, blackest man in Mackerel Sky, Stéphane fell in love with lithe Millicent Stowe, her skin whole milk, her hair cavernous black, and they had a beautiful son the color of caramel.

They were talking about a second baby near the time she drowned.

Stéphane, pronounced like *stay-fawn*, and Millie, rhymes

with *silly*, shared a love of the written word, French (both Parisian and Québecois), silence, and the rituals of the sea. They found comfort in things with depth; they both worked long hours, Stéphane on the waves on his boat, and Millie in the pages in the library. Millie always wanted to write her own book, but she never completed such before she died.

Derrick found comfort in his dad's strong routines and his mother's written words.

In Mackerel Sky, the cave at the foot of High Cliffs, known as the Mermaid's Mouth, is only accessible at low tide. Although Burrbank built his house on the Aerie, many say that the cave was where he hid his treasure, and in the centuries since, the cave has housed many a cache and various secretive deeds. Millie wrote that there Burrbank first spoke to Nimuë. She also wrote that that is where they conceived a baby.

Burrbank would swim on summer days when he felt roots growing out of his feet like worms. He'd swim in the sea recklessly—waves took him under and tossed him back out on the shore, naked, spitting up seawater, and then he'd fling himself back in again like a sacrifice.

Nimuë laughed, and the sound echoed through High Cliffs until it was cut off by an eagle's cry. She was curled up on her favorite stone like a Grecian statue, the water sluicing off her skin. She watched the land-man throw himself against the waves with endless amusement. Her laugh beckoned so he followed, putting on trousers out of propriety though she was naked, her hair covering her breasts with just enough peeka-boo. She let him climb onto her perch.

*"Your name is Captain. I have heard them call you this."
Her voice, the honey and spice of possibility. Her voice, the whisper after sex before sleep. She smiled and shifted slightly toward him, her teeth a choker of pearls.*

"That is one of my names, yes."

"What is another of your names, Captain?" Nimuë, chin lifted, she wore the necklace of her kin, the finest filaments of seaweed fingers woven around a dewy green orb that pulsed with an internal light. Burrbank saw nothing but her. He understood why sailors drowned for a glimpse alone of a mer-row. She pulled him like the tide.

"Yours, if you'll have me." He put his hands on her wet ribs, her wet breasts, and she kissed him on her perch. Her tail split. And under a mackerel sky, the clouds a filet of fish scales, the Captain and the Mermaid consummated their love.

Nine years later, there on Nimuë's Perch, they conceived a child.

Derrick liked that his mother included that Captain Burrbank was naked and the word *peekaboo*, and he wondered about what kind of powers a merbaby would have, and how mermaid sex worked, and what it was like to kiss a mermaid.

Derrick and Ricky kissed secretly all the time now, spring-time, baseball season, birth and rebirth all around. The end of May on a date Ricky led Derrick and Duke along trails through the Skeleton Marshes where the Kingfishers dove. They walked a mile and a half over clapboard bridges slowly being swallowed by the tide. At the marshes, the shallows stretched off in a sandy ribbon. The seawater was warm and clear, and Derrick saw crabs scuttling about and schools of tiny fish. He held Ricky's hand as Ricky nervously, bravely stepped into the water, and then kissed him until Ricky forgot he was standing in the ocean. All wildlife Duke barreled through, and he pranced around the entangled legs of his master and his friend, boys in love on the edge of land and sea.

They kissed in the Mermaid's Mouth at low tide. They kissed at the edge of the ruins of the cursed Lone Dock in the Lone Docks, the cluster of piers and jetties and boat moorings by Low Cliffs.

Thrilling at first, of course, but as dangerous as it was beautiful as it was real, their love spun itself tighter daily, grew life and momentum until it was its own little planet, with its own gravity.

Burrbank built a great pier with the abundant Maine lumber and rooted it in ocean. This was named the Lone Dock. They say the original Lone Dock was cursed on Torch Night in 1721, when Burrbank betrayed Nimuë and the mermaids the third and final time. Boats that docked there sank; people drowned jumping off. Fishermen began avoiding it all together. The dock was dismantled, but a few great logs wouldn't budge and were left pinned to the ocean. These ruins of the original Lone

Dock remained, barnacled and blackened with wet and age and neglect. A new dock was erected next to the skeleton, and eventually a second and third pier were built, and together with the ruins they were known in Mackerel Sky as the Lone Docks. One pier was full of shops, anchored by the Mermaid's Tail Tavern, two were working docks, arms into the sea, and the fourth sat in and out of the ocean, underwater but rooted to land, rotting through history and time.

The second dock was built because the first Lone Dock carried the scorch mark of the mermaids' curse. The dock would henceforth no longer be safe for the harbor. Mermaids can curse the ocean around them, poison it to fish and sailor alike. After Torch Night, and the Third Betrayal, the mermaids cursed the waters around Mackerel Sky. Its bountiful fish harvest dried up and every net came up empty. Boats that once entered and exited port with fine winds and following seas fought sudden gales and whipping brine, the waves mashing on the bows. Burrbank turned away from the sea and to the woods. He found sanctuary in the tall Maine pines, and prospered in timber and masts for ships, and Mackerel Sky grew. But she still haunted him. She would never stop haunting him.

Burrbank was straightforward and smart in nothing involving women, according to the Terror in the Night.

In the middle of cutting down the wildness of the woods, the Piratebird lighted on a birch branch and taught him to replant.

Derrick liked stories about the Piratebird. Some people thought she was part of a witches coven, founded by herself and her wife, a Wabanaki wise woman, to mutually protect the land from the curse of the mermaids. The members of this coven supposedly called themselves Feathers of the Piratebird, descendants of the daughters of Esmeralda Burrbank and of her lover, the Burning Owl. Torch Night, the night Nimuë cursed the town and sent all those residents into the sea, the Feathers of the Piratebird, barefoot in bedclothes, brandishing fire, faced the mermaids as their men were drowning.

Stoic Stéphane, Derrick's father, known in most circles as Blade, had seen many mysteries of the sea that flirted up to the surface, but he had no recollection of ever seeing a mermaid. He did not have time for that noise out on the water; there was work to be done, and distractions caused accidents and accidents caused drownings. He took his work seriously, focused on perfecting routine, trusting that practice made precision and honed efficacy. Blade had seen more than his fair share of fishermen funerals, and he almost gave up the water entirely when it took his wife. But he only lasted as a layman for three months; he was itchy, on edge, couldn't find his balance or the North Star. Only when he returned to his boat, his feet planted on the planks, knees bending with the rocking water below, could he breathe again, did he feel whole. So he went back to lobstering, back to the bounding main.

Millicent Stowe drowned the end of summer, the end of the tourist season. Blade found the most comfort in his routines during this dark, dark time; they served as touchstones, as anchors, as moorings while the grief tossed him with abandon. He had had his established routines as a father, as a husband, as a co-parent, but when Millie died the old world he knew became a flat pane and shattered like glass, and now he navigated school lunches and laundry and doctor's appointments, territory once covered by his wife, alone. Painstakingly, with much trial and error, and bumps and ruts and puddles that blew engines, father and son forged their own path together and grew new routines that became more streamlined each year.

Stéphane kept playbooks of Derrick's baseball games, and he was known for sitting in the stands and writing in them every game he went. He liked to talk stats with the parents and grandparents and teachers that attended. He was loud on occasion, if there was a really bad call, but he was never obnoxious, and he was usually right.

Like his son, he rescued things from the ocean. He had a soft spot for wounded animals, and often sent pregnant lobsters and lobsters too small to catch back into the brink with a fat fish in their claw. He once nursed a seagull back to health, and it lobstered with him for the next four summers. He named it Plum, after an image in a Langston Hughes love poem, a favorite of his and his wife. He buried the bird in their backyard when it flew no more.

He was a good father, stalwart, solid, who spoke little and anchored the ship.

Derrick still had no idea how to tell him he was gay, so he said nothing. On the boat they worked a lot in rhythmic silence, though recently Derrick's thoughts had been very loud.

His mom would have understood. Derrick's memories of her were more faded now, at least eight years old and from when he was young, but they were all warm. She read him books and smoothed back his hair and smelled of lilacs and lavender and the beach. She spoke in soft tones and smiled widely. She swam in the sea like she was born to it.

Derrick learned the rituals of grieving from his father, at eight didn't understand them, at sixteen found comfort in their consistency. He and his father were similar that way; they both were soothed and grounded by ritual. Millie's grave was meticulously clean, always with fresh flowers.

Derrick spoke to his mother at the cemetery, standing over her grave. He went after baseball practice or after school every day.

He told his dead mother all about his boyfriend. He told no one else.

If Derrick were to write about the night he was pummeled to within an inch of his life, his poem would be this:

Oh my heart
They have come to the beach
Carrying confederate flags and torches
the red hats with the white words

Like white walkers
They are drinking and pot-valiant
They will string up the Black men
They will filet the gay
They come for me

Then he would end the poem with a question mark because he thought he was being clever.

. . . They will filet the gay
They come for me
?

Until the Moon, Only Then

*L*eo bit the second corner off his second crabmeat-and-mayonnaise sandwich. He liked to eat both corners first because they had the most bread and that was what he liked to eat the least. His third bite, the best bite, was always front and center, where there was the thickest filling.

He had had inventive sandwiches growing up in the trailer—butter sandwiches and sugar sandwiches and ketchup sandwiches and mayonnaise sandwiches, but never sandwiches like Myra Kelley's. They were filled up and spilled over with ingredients other than expired condiments. The bread was never stale. And he could have as many of them as he wanted.

Full was a feeling he had never felt before, growing up a starving, scrappy kid escaping dark trailers to play Star Wars on the blueberry barrens, where he was always the hero.

He liked the crabmeat one; he told Mrs. Myra once that he liked green olives, and since then she put green olives in his crabmeat sandwiches. He liked that she listened and remembered things he cared about, and how she let him talk and how she was always cooking him things. He liked that her house smelled of the sea and supper and sounded like Dog's steady snores when Leo stayed in the spare room with the messy desk and warm bed.

Myra took the fresh-shucked crabmeat from the blue cooler on her front porch. The cooler had KELLEY written in black Sharpie across the side and always smelled of fish. When Myra's husband, Bernie, found out he was sick, he stood at his roundtable, his truck bed at the wharf, and asked his fisherman friends of decades and days to take care of his Myra. This was unbeknownst to her of course.

One day the cooler showed up packed with ice and fresh haddock and a note that said to leave the cooler outside. The next day there were fresh scallops and the day after four crawling lobsters. Since then the cooler had never been empty. In turn, Myra went down to the wharf on the Paths twice a week to bring homemade goods, whatever extra she cooked, and gave thanks to the hungry mariners coming off the boats.

And there at the shore she heard stories of Bernie, stories she knew well, stories she knew differently, stories she didn't know at all. She saw the *Laughing Lamb*, Bernie's boat that she sold to his loyal sternman, Oswald. He'd take Myra out on the boat every now and then, anytime. It was an offer that still held from the time they were fifteen.

Leo went into Myra's living room. He liked the living room, with big windows wide to the ocean and shelves of shells and leather-bound books. The two couches each had an afghan hung over the edge and thick pillows that Leo and Dog got lost in. The red book sat on its pedestal, and it was open today, for the first time in a long while, the dust mites frolicking in the late-day sunlight over its pages.

Leo walked to it reverently. "Miss Myra! The book's open!"

"Is it, now? Land sakes." Myra sounded genuinely surprised. "It opened for you, then. You best read it."

Leo didn't know what Myra meant, of course she herself opened the book, but she was old and old people forgot things sometimes, and Leo didn't need to be told to look at what he had been wanting to look at for weeks.

The book was very old, the pages yellowing, and had many different authors. The script changed, the inks were different, the dates crossed time. Rudimentary maps of the Paths that connected the land of Mackerel Sky evolved in complexity and detail over pages. Leo saw some footpaths had widened to become roads, some footpaths extended into the docks on the sea, some were dirt trails over rock crags on land into ocean. Some ran parallel to the main road in the woods, some escaped to the outskirts of town through the woods to the flat June green of the blueberry barrens months from harvest. They intersected; they diverged; they slinked; they linked the town like green twine in a fishing net. Leo recognized Paths he had run over and over. He traced his finger over the Path he and Myra walked regularly to High Cliffs, and he could have sworn he saw a shimmery gold trail follow his finger all the way across the page until he turned it. When he flipped the page back, to look at the map again, the map had disappeared, and he couldn't find what page it was on.

As he flipped through the book, he saw it contained clippings from old newspapers, articles about hurricanes and blizzards and weddings and deaths with titles such as "A Mournful Remembrance of the Much to be Lamented Death of the Worthy and Pious." Myra's wedding picture was there, she in her white wedding dress and Bernie in his uniform right before he shipped off to England to war.

A gilded family tree had been drawn on both inside covers. It dated well past Burrbank, noting his marriage to both Esmeralda and Nimuë, as well as his children: Tristolde, born to Burrbank and the Mermaid in 1720, and Ariadne, born to Burrbank and Esmeralda in 1723. Some tree limbs ended with the word *deceased*, some ended with what looked like waves. Burrbank's ended with a question mark.

"My mom's in this book? And Mrs. Perle? *I'm* in this book, Miss Myra! Wait, I'm related to fucking *Burrbank*?"

"Watch that mouth. Ayuh. Your mother is my cousin's great-niece. On my mother's side."

"Wow! That makes us related somehow."

"Somehow."

One branch ended with Myra's two babies—deceased, deceased.

"Miss Myra—your real name is Lorelei?"

"Ayuh, kid, but that's my Sunday name, or when I'm in trouble." Only Bernie had called her Lorelei.

"I'm sorry about your babies, Miss Myra. That must have been wicked sad."

And though it had been over fifty years, her arms ached, her breasts ached for those babies never held.

"It was, the wickedest sadness. They didn't take a breath in this world. Thanks, Leo boy."

He hugged her then, tight around the waist. It surprised them both, but they both settled in well.

He returned to the book.

"Don't get any crabmeat on those pages," Myra Kelley warned.

There were sketches of mermaids. Leo stopped short.

"That one. That one looks a lot like the one I saw. Different colors though."

Myra walked over silently. He pointed to a soft-skinned, raven-haired beauty lounging luxuriously on a rock, her tail half in the ocean. Leo looked at the signature in the corner.

"Holy shi—*shoot*, Miss Myra—Burrbank *himself* drew this?"

"Yes he did. There are many of his sketches in this book. There is a book full of his sketches somewhere in the Christmas cabinet, but it's hiding."

"Hiding? Books can hide?"

"Mm," hummed Myra indistinctly. She scrutinized the drawing. "That's Nimuë, the mermaid he loved."

"So Burrbank drew this—so mermaids *are* real? I wasn't crazy?"

"No, not crazy, but I think you need to stay away from the coffee brandy, boy."

Leo scoffed. "Come on, Miss Myra. Do you believe in the mermaids? Are they real? Have you seen one?"

"I believe there are things in the ocean I don't know about. I don't know what I don't know."

Leo slumped. "That's not an answer."

Myra smiled and pinched his chin. "It's going to have to do."

"Miss Myra—" Leo began.

"Enough red book today, boy. You done your work?"

Leo resigned. "Yes, Miss Myra."

"Okay, then, let's walk the Paths. Dog needs to go outside." Leo and Myra habitually walked the Paths together after dinner after he worked on her barn. Leo looked at Dog, who was sleeping in the sun. He farted and snored.

"I don't think he really wants a walk, Miss Myra." Leo looked back at the red brocaded book. It was closed. He didn't remember closing it.

"Dog don't know what's good for him sometimes. Besides,

I need to go to the wharf to drop off these crabby patties."
She had mixed crabmeat with old English cheese and broiled
it on top of English muffins, a favorite among Mackerel Sky's
fishermen.

"They done?" Leo brightened.

Myra smiled and sighed. "Yes, kid. There's a paper plate
on the kitchen table for you. Go grab it for our walk. When
you're finished you can carry the crabby patties for me."

Leo bounced and did what he was told.

Jason Perle came up after work again that day to help with
the barn and then toss a Frisbee with Dog and Leo. They
all gathered around Myra's kitchen table with the wobbly
leg for a fish-fry supper, Dog's head on Leo's knees. Jason,
in between bites, told Mrs. Myra he was getting the better
deal in the bargain.

"Not a bargain, a gentleman's agreement," Leo corrected him.

After dinner (and dessert) Jason taught Leo how to fix the
leg of the table and then went home to his empty house with
two of three bedrooms unused, and one gathering dust behind
a closed door. He'd usually take the Paths and wander to the
Lone Docks and the shore and sit in the stern of his ship in
its slip and watch the stars.

Leo and Myra walked Dog on the Paths crisscrossing
Mackerel Sky. The Paths had no official signs, only markers
passed generation to generation. Some of the main thorough-
fares in Mackerel Sky were veins of the original Paths and had
become Beacon Street, Main Street, Route 1. Many however

were still just worn ruts through the grass and lupines and Queen Anne's lace.

Sometimes Leo and Myra walked to the wharf at the Lone Docks, sometimes to Crescent Beach. Often they walked to Burrbank's Leap on the Aerie at High Cliffs. Myra would stop and stare at the waves for a while from next to a long oblong stone. Then she would throw a single egg over the side. Leo liked throwing things over the side too, so he threw rocks and sticks. He once asked her why she threw the egg.

"Are you getting back at the chickens?"

"No, Leo. I'm paying tribute."

"Tribute? To who?"

"Atargatis."

Leo just nodded his head because he didn't know what any of it meant, and he didn't want to look like he didn't know what any of it meant.

The egg-throwing walk became one of their rituals. Leo was okay with it; old people were weird. He liked the edge of High Cliffs. He felt like he was on the edge of the world.

One night Leo was up late reading by lamplight eating a peanut butter and fluff sandwich and heard a thump in the living room. It was late, Myra had already gone to bed, and he and Dog raced to explore the sound, but nothing was amiss in the living room, though a candle was lit, and the red brocaded book was open. Dog nudged him forward and then nuzzled his big head under the boy's hand as he walked toward the book. It was open to another page that he hadn't seen before, with the tea-colored flowing script he had come to identify as Burrbank's.

> *Until the moon, full, drips down*
> *After a bloodstained mackerel sky*
> *Until a brother for a brother, waves round*
> *Until the lines are crossed, wayfarer by*
> *Until a daughter for a son, both of rock, both of wave*
> *Until the twin pearls together return,*
> *Until a mother for a mother, one lost, one saved*
> *Twin hearts to forever burn*
> *Only then*

It looked like the poem faded away, was incomplete.

He knew about the mermaids' curse of Mackerel Sky. Everyone knew about it, whether they believed in it or not. They say Burrbank betrayed the mermaid Nimuë the third and final time by keeping their baby Tristolde to be raised by him on the land. Her son taken from her, her brother strangled and his birthright stolen, her man in love with the Piratebird, enraged, broken-hearted, bereft, Nimuë and her mermaid brethren cursed Mackerel Sky and sent eight residents into the drink.

Ever since that night, Mackerel Sky had had more drownings and young fishermen lost to the sea than any town up and down the seaboard, though most people chalked that up to weather or equipment or drinking, not a three-hundred-year-old mermaid curse.

Leo understood parts of the poem but not all of it. He understood a "moon, full" meant a full moon, of course. He knew what a mackerel sky looked like, when the clouds swam across the sky in little white bursts like fish scales, and "bloodstained" could mean after a battle or a red sky at morning, sailors take warning. But twin pearls? He didn't get it. He didn't get it but he liked it, so he whispered it out loud in the flickering flame, imagining he was a wizard incanting. This was his spell. He called it "Until the Moon, Only Then" to help him remember it.

By the next week he had it memorized and was whispering it or chanting it or singing it on their walks on the Paths until Myra asked him to tone it down. She did that rarely, though. A boy singing was always a good thing.

". . . until the moon, only then . . ."

"Enough, now, boy. Be careful with your words. It's important."

"What's important?"

"What you say out loud is important. Your word reflects who you are."

Leo hit at some bushes with a long stick.

"Okay. Miss Myra, I'm really happy I ran into your barn and didn't die."

"Me too, kid."

"I mean, I'm real sorry too, but I'm glad I got to hang out with you. Can I throw the egg this time?"

"You throw it the farthest."

Leo nodded in agreement, so it was decided.

They walked to the edge of High Cliffs, to the rock outcropping where Myra chased Leo to that night in March. It looked a lot different in the daylight and late spring, all green and blue and sparkling, the bald eagles nesting in their pine. Leo threw the egg as hard as he could, and it landed far in the waves. Myra always cheered, and Leo always smiled.

"My get-up-and-go got up and went," remarked Myra after they returned, chewing her pipe in her front porch rocking chair.

"Can I stay here again tonight, Miss Myra?" he asked, opening the cooler. Today there were brook trout.

"Boy, you can stay here as long as you need. Spare room's all made up. Help yourself to the fridge—there's extra dinner. And stuff for sandwiches."

"Thanks, Miss Myra."

Leo hadn't heard from his mother in weeks and so had been staying almost daily with Myra. His mother didn't reach out or reach back to him. She hadn't been home at the trailer. She did this sometimes, left him for weeks. Once, when he was eight, she was gone for nine days. Starving, he burned his arm on the stove trying to make instant mashed potatoes. He took care of the staggering wound himself. He told this story to Myra, and she pursed her lips and bit her pipe but kept the bad words at bay. That night Leo ate chocolate chip cookies hot from the oven, baked just for him. Myra called the large ugly scar a battle wound for a strong soldier. He liked that. It made him feel better about not being able to make mashed potatoes and about how his mother didn't love him.

When Leo opened the refrigerator he smiled, because there were two sandwiches with turkey falling out the sides already made for him. Dog nudged his hand, for he had seen them too.

Wicked Pretty

*N*imue Perle died a little less than six months after her fourth birthday. It was a golden late afternoon, early August, during high festivities of the Mermaid Festival.

Mackerel Sky's celebrated three-day Mermaid Festival was born entirely by accident in 1903 and had grown in size and popularity every year since. Supposedly, a rich sea captain named Robert Smith, a far descendant of Ariadne Burrbank, retired to Mackerel Sky after sailing circles around the world. He returned to port from the coast of Wales, where he had vacationed on Llandudno and spent much of his leisure time on its great pier, where he enjoyed the little pubs and his first Punch and Judy puppet show. Smith always thought in grand strokes, and watching the laughing children and parents toss coins in a coffer for puppets while the water sparkled behind them got him thinking; he saw no reason why Mackerel Sky's Lone Docks couldn't be as lucrative and inviting.

In the center of the second Lone Dock, Bob erected a puppet theater, and painted it with white and red stripes, and his wife darned the puppets—cotton-stuffed fabric caricatures of the legend of Mackerel Sky: Captain Burrbank and his infamous crew, Nimuë and her mermaids, the Piratebird, and the Wabanaki. Every weekend in the summer the two of them, Bob and Sally Smith, husband and wife, squished themselves behind the curtain of the puppet theater and reenacted the battles of Burrbank and the pirates and of Mackerel Sky and the mermaids. Small crowds began gathering.

That same summer in 1903, a discovery was made in the marshes that put Mackerel Sky on the map for tourists who had never heard of it, which was, frankly, every tourist. That summer had been particularly dry; the grasses were as yellow and spiky and desperate as they normally were mid-August, and yet it was only mid-July. The heat had dried up the duck pond near Myra Kelley's into three fat separate pools rapidly evaporating into puddles. The marshes near the Lone Docks and Low Cliffs, drier than they ever had been, coughed up secrets long suffocated in the wet sands, including, one Sunday afternoon during the Smiths' Mermaid and Pirate Punch and Judy show, a skeleton, with the upper torso of a human, arms unfurled to the sun. At first when they pulled the body out of the muck they thought the legs had been broken off, but upon further examination found the lower half oddly coiled; the bones thin and many and veined into a V, much like the lower tail of a fish, some said.

Myra Kelley's red book contained the newspaper article describing the discovery of the mer-fossil in the marshes: "Wicked Pretty: Strange Tides and Tidings from Mackerel Sky, Maine," with a grainy daguerreotype of the skeleton, curled like a cut conch shell, like the golden rectangle. Thrill-seekers and nay-sayers and curio-collectors flocked to the little port-side town, filling the Ink and Crane and any local guesthouse or inn that would have them. Men who had known nothing but the rugged Maine coast and her sea offered, for a price, "Mermaid Water Tours Extraordinaire" to the wealthy tourists with parasols and pinafores hoping for a mermaid sighting. The fishermen loaded landlubbers up next to their bait and rigging, in dories and skiffs, and took the tourists for a ride out on the water. They joined the Saturday and Sunday crowds of children and tossed coins into the Smiths' Punch and Judy show. Bob Smith also gathered a ragtag group of amateur thespians, and they mounted a production in three days entitled *Mermaids and Mackerel Sky: A True History* and acted out the legend of Burrbank and Nimuë and the Piratebird with much gusto and little experience. At night the sailors told tales over ales in the pub, the later in the night the larger the fish, each fisherman sharing a greater story of a mermaid encounter than the fisherman before.

And for one hour each day, the mer-skeleton was displayed, in a glass case behind a velvet curtain that was wheeled out onto the second Lone Dock.

Soon the horseshit of the vacationing wealthy was too much for Mackerel Sky's cobweb of Paths, soon the seamen needed to return to the sea to fish, not look for mermaids, and the Mackerel Sky's dying mayor became tired of the ruckus and the rigor and considered tossing the bones back into the benthos to be done with it. But Bob Smith and his wife, Sally, and their small, stalwart group of fishermen/actors suggested that perhaps Mackerel Sky could share the mer-skeleton with the tourists once per year, and the Mackerel Sky Mermaid Festival was born.

Traditions become rooted when they are well-watered by the people, and the festival shoot grew and sprouted new branches and leaves and blooms over the years to become the ancient oak it was in the Mackerel Sky community today: a three-day festival with pageants, fireworks, bake-offs, quilt-offs, the Mermaid Parade down Beacon and Main Streets, music in the gazebo, lobster-boat races, food trucks, and tents, tents, tents—for crafts, for food, for games, for dancing, for sitting—all of which took a year of planning and multiple committees to manage.

The Mermaid of Skeleton Marshes disappeared the third

year of the nascent Mermaid Festival—stolen, hidden, no official record on who took it—and thus it moved from the tangible world into legend and became myth in Mackerel Sky.

Every year, on one of the three days of the Mermaid Festival, someone drowned, always. Tourists tended to be easier prey, but that was not always the case.

At one point little Nimue Perle was in the stern of the lobster boat and the next she wasn't—Deaddeer's words; but he was two boats over and well into his first thirty-pack.

On Nimue's boat, the *Pearl*, captained by her father, Jason, enough passengers confirmed that she died in her mother's arms, on her mother's lap, wrapped in her crocheted fish-scale blanket, headed home from a clambake on Iledest Island, the water calm and steadily blackening. No one saw how she disappeared off the stern.

"When the whale breached, when the eagle landed, I gave her to the mermaid. She asked me to do it. You would have too, my love," Manon told Jason. "But you were at the helm. You didn't see. You didn't see. You didn't see."

The general consensus at the IGA was that Manon Perle went crazy that very day. She fell into an abyss and no one could find her, not her husband, not herself.

Jason navigated the oceans; they were more predictable.

The doctors at the sanatorium told Manon to stop believing in mermaids.

"But I would stop believing if I could. That day on the water; that day she died on my lap; she was alive and I looked and there was a whale coming out of the water. Then my little mermaid stopped breathing. She wouldn't start again. When shit like that happens, you stop believing in mermaids because believing in mermaids is believing in magic and hope, and magic and hope could not possibly exist simultaneously in *a world where your fucking baby dies in your fucking lap*. Don't you understand? I don't want to believe in mermaids. But I have to. I gave my baby to one."

Manon was sedated often.

When Manon and Jason were dating they often went to a lake about an hour by bike past the end of Beacon Street, past the blueberry barrens into the woods. Manon had a favorite flat rock in a cove that she had been swimming to since she could swim. Jason followed her and they kissed wet in the sunlight. For other dates they went on the ocean; they took Jason's boat to moor off the back shore of Iledest Island and stayed on the boat and swam or searched for treasures washed ashore.

They had loved each other for a long time.

Jason fell first and furiously for Manon the long-haired, the long-legged, with a smile like the horizon, like relief.

When Manon moved into the apartment above the Three Bats and the waves, she kept her wedding album packed in a box in her bedroom. She didn't have the heart to look at it or the heart to throw it away. She and Jason were all but divorced. They had yet to file paperwork; Jason wouldn't think to and the only papers that Manon could handle were the creative writings by her students and sometimes her bills.

The Sisters always asked about Jason.

"How's that handsome young man of yours, dear?" Gladys might say. They pronounced dear *dee-yah* and didn't miss a stitch. When Manon didn't answer, they did for her.

"Still being foolish I see." Beatrix this time. Stitching and rocking.

"Ayuh." Agathe-Alice. Agathe-Alice, always wrapped up in blankets in her wheelchair.

The Three Bats preferred to sit overlooking the comings and goings of the port. They shared the only house on the Lone Docks. Manon moved into an apartment above them, and one night joined their knitting and sewing with one of her quilts. They welcomed her without missing a stitch, and most evenings she sewed with them. Each of the Sisters now had her own quilt, gifts from Manon, wrapped about their legs. Each quilt told the tale of Mackerel Sky and the Mermaid in nine panels, works of art, all.

The quilt of Agathe-Alice was sewn with all the ripples of blue of the ocean, the prow of Nimuë always settling at the bend in her knees. Beatrix draped herself in the briny greens while she stitched knot after knot into nets commissioned by some of the more seasoned seamen who swore up and down the seaboard that somehow her nets snagged more catch. The background fabric for Gladys's quilt was a kaleidoscope of fire; it matched the speed of her knitting needles and the blaze of her eyes.

Some nights Manon sat and sewed silent until sunset, and the old ladies sat chattering around her, asking her questions and then answering for her, almost always correctly.

The Three Bats understood stitching oneself back together. They had seen many lifetimes of their own.

Manon broke mirrors the first week in the asylum; shattered mirror on the floor, the girl who lived here lives no more. In her white room, Manon dreamed of Jason at the edge of the shore, the sand sinking him to hold on to him as the water lapped and pulled him away. She dreamed of her dead daughter submerging into the sea.

Jason found solace in the ocean instead of her; he took his boat, the *Pearl*, to a place she couldn't reach. Jason thought a lot about that sound she made that day on the boat, a wounded, final throe, the sound of a heart shattering to sand. He saw the little gray cold face of his daughter and then tried to stop thinking.

The grief grew like a wall of fog between them, and Jason and Manon lost each other, alone with their exiles.

For a long time after Nimue died, after Nimue's cenotaph was placed in the Evergreen Cemetery, after Manon was institutionalized a couple times, Manon still absently bought her daughter's old favorite groceries. Nimue loved red grapes. Manon didn't enjoy grapes, but she had a bottom drawer filled with red grapes in various stages of decomposition.

Then she saw a picture of a dead spider in a bag of red grapes online. She compulsively searched for the spiders in her grapes because she could not stop buying little Nimue red grapes. She could find none.

Spiders could be creepy. Invisible spiders were terrifying.

Manon was institutionalized the second time when she was again deemed a danger to herself. She had been found multiple times lying in skiffs and drifting in the ocean. Fishermen would come upon her lying like Ophelia in the hull, rolling in the swells.

Jason found her. Stéphane too, many times.

"Did you get lost again today, Manon?" Stéphane pronounced her name the French way, *mah-no*, when he tossed her the rope. Sometimes she'd say yes, sometimes she'd smile, sometimes she would continue staring into the water as if she was looking for something. Sometimes he would ask her in French.

"Perdue, Manon?" *Lost, Manon?*

"Toujours." *Always.*

"It happens to the best of us," he said, handing her a blanket, remembering his wife's death and the grief that eclipsed him. He too scanned the ocean like she did, like sonar. Sometimes, while out on the water, he had an unshakable feeling that he had lost something, or forgotten something, but the feeling passed by the time he reached the shore.

Alone on the Three Bats' porch at sunrise, Manon sewed a quilt for Stéphane and his son, Derrick, in thanks. The Three

Bats didn't come out to sew until after their lunchtime nap, but Manon liked to watch the sunrise. She liked to watch the sky burn steady and fierce, burn away everything bad from yesterday.

Manon had stockpiled ten quilts to sell at this year's Mermaid Festival in August. She would ask for one thousand apiece and she would get it. She would donate the eleventh quilt to the auction; each year her auctioned quilt fetched a hefty sum for the town and that year's charity.

She didn't do it for the money. She just stitched herself back together, because sometimes the sound of thread through fabric was louder than the grief.

Burrbank's Leap was an outcropping of rocks at the edge of High Cliffs. It was so named because Captain Burrbank disappeared off the peak twenty years after he first made port in Mackerel Sky. One twilight he simply strode off into the night, telescope in hand, toward High Cliffs, and was never seen again.

The consensus was that he'd leapt into the sea.

Some thought he saw his love the Mermaid again and dove to be with her; some believed he never saw Nimuë again and despaired. Some thought he was chased, by Esmeralda's priestess lover and her women's battalion. Some thought he and his crew commandeered a vessel and stole away into the night, perhaps the mermaids caught them and drowned them in the drink, perhaps Burrbank and his crew were now statues forever tethered to the bottom in Davy Jones's locker.

Manon never went near High Cliffs. She preferred the Lone Docks and Low Cliffs and Crescent Beach and the Skeleton Marshes, or floating aimlessly in the ocean. She preferred anywhere to the rock's edge where Burrbank disappeared in the night. She wasn't afraid of heights, no, she was afraid of suddenly throwing herself off into the stars, like the Captain, a moment of whirling sea air, the sky and sea mirroring each other in the night, a thousand constellations on the waves, before she was swallowed by dark water and became memory.

The Book Burner

The morning of the Book Burner the sunrise spread across the sky as smoldering wildfire; the black silhouettes of boats cut into the morning's canvas like claw marks.

Derrick turned his pillow over to the cool side and saw nothing of that morning's sunrise. His father Blade did, though, and viewed it with thin lips and furrowed brow.

That morning Manon was surprised the see the Sisters already awake and wrapped in their quilts on their rocking chairs watching the sky bloom pink. They weren't stitching but sat looking at the sky, all wrapped in the same huge quilt that once was black but had been so faded by years and sun it was pale blue in places, like a robin's egg. Embroidered across the quilt like capillaries or netting or spiderwebs were thin golden lines of thread, filaments that the Three Bats were each tracing with a finger. They seemed to be mumbling something, but when Manon came closer they stopped.

"Red sky at morning," said Beatrix, her finger still following the thread.

"Sailors better take fucking warning," spat Gladys, two hands on the quilt, eyes staring down the sunrise.

"Including that handsome husband of yours, though he is a Mackerel Sky fisherman, so odds are doubtful." Agathe-Alice smiled over her immobile legs. "They are some twitchy today."

The fog rolled in then, separate strands of steam furling and unfurling and stretching across the land in slow tongues. The ocean became part of the land, enveloping it in wet white, unlikely to burn off, blurring the boundary between land and sea.

The Book Burner was a bonfire that took place the night of the last day of school in June on Crescent Beach near Mermaid's Mouth. Dark to dawn the high school students drank warm light beer and thick, sweet coffee brandy with soda and cream, trading cigarettes and memories and saliva. The last party of the school year, the first party of the summer, students lit their school assignments ablaze. Legend said mermaids were terrified of fire, and beaches safer when bonfires were lit.

Every generation had a cautionary tale about how a student nearing graduation had died at this event—drowned drunk in the ocean, fell down the stairway from High Cliffs, got caught in Mermaid's Mouth at high tide.

This year's Book Burner would be known as the night Derrick Stowe died.

Due to his pitching popularity, Derrick had been attending the Book Burner since he was in eighth grade. He tried a cigarette stolen from his friend's mother that year and got drunk-sick for the first time the next year. He usually brought his dog Duke with him, but this year he decided not to because he wanted to be able to sneak away at any moment—Ricky would be meeting him there, his secret date.

No one knew about his clandestine, perfect, adorable boyfriend save for his dog and dead mother and the ink in his journals. Sometimes Derrick thought his father knew something was different, that something was changed; Stéphane would stare at his son searchingly, and Derrick would reward him with silence. Derrick felt that his father was waiting, paddock gate open, waiting for him to come out of his own accord. Derrick felt like a coward. The truth bubbled painfully in his chest, lying in wait, eager to pounce.

Derrick and Ricky had been seeing each other for six

months now. They attended story hour at the Millcreek Library, where Derrick read. They walked the Paths with Duke and picnicked in the cemetery at his mother's grave. They went to Crescent Beach and Ricky waded in the water a bit farther every time. Derrick read words from his mother's journals, from her research on the myths of mermaids of Mackerel Sky. Ricky loved it; he was a history fanatic, especially obscure heroes and untold stories.

For a mermaid, a bird's egg is a rare, exotic treat from the land. Most mermaids have never seen nor felt the air; some do not even believe in it. So to learn that there are creatures that have mastered the art of swimming in the nothing, to learn that there are creatures who surf the currents of the wind, is an astonishing fact indeed for merfolk.

These magical creatures come from water, form from yolk, and break through their universe to be. Their eggs, tiny oceans encapsulated by shell, to become a being of the air, earth, fire, and water, all.

The first eggs mermaids tried were those of puffins, or terns, or gulls, birds that nested near the waves. But if a sailor seeks to charm a mermaid, or seek her favor, he must bring goose eggs or chicken eggs or pheasant eggs upon his boat, eggs that mermaids cannot catch with their own hands unless they come upon the shore, and place two into the sea before he fishes for a bountiful catch.

"Really? Mermaids like eggs?" Ricky laughed heartily. It was one of Derrick's most favorite sounds in the world.

Ricky came to some of Derrick's baseball games. He would have gone to all of them, but he didn't want to raise suspicion regarding their relationship.

Jared and Colby Townsend had never seen their annoying little shit brother so busy, so social, so happy. He was even going near the water again, which he had sworn off after they threw him from the skiff one time and realized—almost too late—that he couldn't swim. It didn't sit right with them or their father, to see that faggoty little fuck prancing around when money was tight, and the government and the Man had taken away Dad's license so he couldn't drive to work no more.

"Selfish little prick," Roy Townsend spat at his twin sons, reiterating that their brother Ricky was a worthless piece of trash.

For their fifth-month anniversary Derrick gave Ricky the green pearl necklace that Myra Kelley had given him after his mother died. Ricky never took it off.

Derrick wrote in his journal about one of their dates:

> *Something about the light*
> *Of a candle*
> *How it changes a room*
> *into history*
> *Or a conversation*
> *into something deeper*

It brings all these molecules
That bump us and kiss us and skip us and flatten us
into a boardroom and says
Here's some mulled cider
And a fleece blanket
Calm your asses down

He titled the poem "Candlelight."

* * *

Derrick was in love for the first time in his life.

Derrick filled an empty Moxie bottle with dark rum from his father's liquor cabinet and replaced half of what he took with water. His father hardly drank, and Derrick rarely stole booze, so his father never noticed that his liquor was lighter. He kissed his pet Duke's stinky, fluffy head, but left him home, whining by the door.

He arrived at the Book Burner after sunset and took a healthy pull off the bottle and then a healthy pull of Ricky, who was playing guitar with three Mermaids, three cheer-leaders who were sipping off cider and requesting songs half gone and half in the bag.

He plays songs for me, Dad, just me. Like you used to sing to Mom. I read poetry to him, Dad, like Mom used to read to you. I read him mine, words that I am afraid to read to anyone.

The baseball team calls me Rembrandt because I paint the

corners with my pitches, my boyfriend calls me Coffee Bean,
because he thinks my skin is beautiful, and my skin is yours and
Mom's.

I am so in love.

He thought all these things while looking directly in Ricky's eyes and could swear Ricky thought them too especially right there, right then, in the small-town firelight.

Jared Townsend saw them look at each other too, but his thoughts were vitriol.

They say on Torch Night Nimuë of the Deep came to Mackerel Sky pregnant with vengeance under an eclipsed blood moon. She was irate that Burrbank had begun courting Esmeralda and devastated that her brother had been strangled to death by one of the nets of Burrbank's men. But that night she came for her child. She rode the crest of oily black waters fissured with foam. The waves chomped on the land, snapping off pieces and swallowing them whole. That night eight men drowned.

Derrick told this to Ricky, close to his ear.

In the fog, Derrick and Ricky thought they had gotten far enough from the party that they were completely alone. They thought they were safe.

They say the wind that came with Nimuë on Torch Night in 1721 gathered up everything not grounded and spat it out like shrapnel, shredding home and mast and tree. The ocean raged, waves churning, whirlpools opening like throats. Nimuë rode the crest of a tidal wave. She came for Burrbank. She came for her son.

The mermaids began to sing.

Lightning struck and set the town on fire.

The Feathers of the Piratebird came out of the town and the woods along the coast, some barefoot, ready to fight, torches in hand. They knew mermaids were terrified of fire. The pioneers of Mackerel Sky would burn the town down if they had to, before they let it be taken by the sea. Up and down Crescent Beach the Feathers lit fires in the sand, using boards from houses to feed them, a warning for the maidens in the waves. The Piratebird rescued Burrbank's coffer before setting his house ablaze.

"What is the feathers of the what?" Ricky asked, in between kissing.

The height of the party, the flames sparked and the tops popped. The fog evaporated into the night, and the moon came out full and pink like a period.

Derrick kissed Ricky for the last time.

He pulled back to admire his love, a few buttons undone, his shirt opened to his bare chest, resting on his back, the cave dripping. Derrick rubbed his eyes because he swore the green pearl in Ricky's necklace was glowing.

"What the *fuck*?"

The voice was not theirs. And it was outraged.

Jared Townsend, seasoned Book Burner drunk, processed

what he saw bits at a time: his brother Ricky, chest out, under the pitcher Derrick, in Mermaid's Mouth, right where he was going to take a piss.

"What the *fuck*?" He was comprehending now, the stare at the bonfire, his brother always out, his brother so happy, splashing in the water. He was backing away, panic bubbling. Derrick and Ricky sprang apart. Jared started screaming for his other brother.

And the liquor told Jared and Colby what it told their father and his father before him and his father before that.

Rage.

Nowhere as Alone

*D*uring the famous Mermaid Festival every August, after the Mermaid Parade down Beacon Street, Manon and Jason and Nimue and a smattering of friends and family members gathered on Jason's lobster boat for the annual lobster-boat races and a cookout on the back shore of Iledest Island.

Four years ago the revelers were wrapped in blankets and beach towels and each other's arms. In the stern, Nimue was wrapped in her favorite blanket sewn by the Three Bats and sat on her mother's lap. She was a whole four years old and a big girl. She wore the lone pearl earring from Mrs. Kelley, and her Mermaid Princess tiara from starring on her own float in the parade, and the blanket from her three Auntie Bats that looked like a sparkly fish tail. They were leaving the island, sunbaked and tired, watching the waves, drawn in to the lull of the boat. The water was dark, the sky apricot, the clouds fish scales.

Manon now only lived that moment in her dreams, the moment before her world broke apart and a part of her psyche went into exile. Only at night, in her dreams, when she had no control, no power, did she relive that moment, when her daughter was alive and then not, when her daughter's soul pulled away from its body as gently as a cobweb and was gone.

The storm came out of nowhere.

Manon began screaming.

The waves got rough, and the wind picked up. A humpback whale breached.

The partygoers grabbed the sides and tumbled about, splashed by the break, tossed by the valleys.

Manon was still screaming.

Nimue had stopped breathing and turned blue.

Portside the humpback breached again.

Courtney, family friend and a nurse, examined the little girl in between lurches.

Fatal cardiovascular deformities are often a symptom of sirenomelia, and Nurse Courtney stated that little Nimue

Perle's heart simply stopped that day. She took a nap on her mother and never woke up.

How she died was never the controversy.

Manon spoke rarely at group therapy in the asylums. The first time she told the story of her daughter's death she did so in monotone and completely disassociated.

"I always told Nimue she was part mermaid, to help her cope with her sadness about being different from the other kids. She had her own mermaid float in the parade. I saw a mermaid in the water that day she died. The sea was wild, different shades of gray. The mermaid's hair and skin were the color of seaweed. She asked me to give her Nimue. My daughter was a mermaid. She had to go back to the ocean. So I did. I gave her back to the ocean."

There was nowhere as alone as Manon and her dead daughter on that stern. The tears came in such a steady stream that she became a tributary to the ocean.

When the whale breached again, this time off the starboard bow, Manon, cradling Nimue, saw a mermaid in the water, reaching up to her from below the surface, reaching for her dead daughter.

Manon thought of Antoine de Saint-Éxupery, and his quote "Quand le mystère est trop impressionnant, on n'ose pas désobéir."

When the mystery is so incredible, one dares not disobey.

She thought, *My daughter is dead.*

So she leaned over the stern in the cadence of the crests

and let her daughter go. The lifeless child passed through the ocean's surface, a mirror pane of sea and sky, like the painting of the divine touch in the Sistine Chapel. The blanket was still wrapped around her legs. Under the water, as Nimue was held by the mermaid, her clothes disappeared. Air bubbles bloomed under the blanket. Scales shot down her fused legs like bubbling paint in a house fire, like a mermaid tail was forming.

Then her eyes were white marbles in the dark, then ascending bubbles, then black.

In therapy, later, doctors would call these hallucinations. Manon didn't want to believe they were right. She wanted to believe her daughter turned into a mermaid.

When Jason turned back and his baby girl had disappeared, he started screaming.

The waves began to calm, and a sobbing Manon peeled herself off the stern onto Courtney's knees. Courtney held and rocked her as Manon wailed out her shattered heart. Jason tried to jump in the water, but it was clearly too late and his best friend held him back until his struggles led to his tears.

Deaddeer was day drunk, but his boat was first to come to their aid. The coast guard came later.

There was nothing they could do.

At baby Nimue's birth and just after baby Nimue's death, the winters were harsh. When she was born, Mackerel Sky was buried in feet of snow and ice, and four years later the winter brought a punishing cold that drove people into their houses to sit with mugs and whirling thoughts.

Manon kept the pearl earring that the murder of crows had found for her. She kept it on her person and played with it in her left pocket. Nimue would have been so happy to have found it; she wore its mate faithfully until her death. They took Nimue's pearl earring from her mother in the mental hospital, and she screamed and screamed a wet howl until she needed to be sedated again.

Manon stayed in the hospital for thirty days the first time. She took a car directly from the funeral. Jason tried to visit with her, tried to talk to her, but the fog of their grief was so enveloping they couldn't see each other through it anymore.

"Throw it all away," she said of Nimue's belongings, her toys, her books. "She won't need it anymore. Throw it all away."

He didn't, and her four-year-old bedroom stayed intact and closed, steadily graying and fading under dust and sunshine.

She would describe her grief not as madness anymore. Now her madness was deciphering what was real and what was insanity. The doctors kept telling her she had them switched. Her baby died. Her baby was not a mermaid.

But Manon saw her small form descending down down down to the deep, held in the arms of a merrow under the surface. It brought her peace to think of Nimue as a mermaid, even if the doctors told her it wasn't true.

She wished Jason had believed her. She still remembered his face that day when she told him in their bedroom that she gave their dead child to a mermaid.

"*What?*" he said, incredulous. His hand went through his hair. "What the actual *fuck*, Manon?"

To this day she didn't know if he believed her. She didn't know if she believed herself, because all the doctors kept telling her she was wrong. To be welcomed back into the fold of humanity, perhaps to heal, she wanted to tell the doctors what they wanted to hear, that mermaids weren't real; that her daughter wasn't taken among them, but every night when she closed her eyes she saw Nimue in the arms of the mermaid, descending into the deep, fish scales erupting on her legs with the speed of a fire on a brush plain.

Manon would always be drawn to the water. She was always looking for Nimue.

Remnants of Burrbank's house still stood on the Aerie. He built his house on the cliffs to have the best vantage point of the town and the sea. There he raised his son, Tristolde. Esmeralda became his wife and moved into his rebuilt home, two years after she burned it down. They had a daughter, Ariadne.

From his perch Burrbank spent many a morning and evening surveying the land and the waters. He would always look for Nimuë.

Manon at the water, playing with the pearl earring in her pocket, always looking for her little girl.

Why must we all die? she thought, over and over. And then, *I miss her. I miss holding her so much.* Then she stared into the waves until her mind drowned in them.

Manon listened to music, gazing out the window, especially at night, when she lit a candle in case Nimue needed the light to come home. Sometimes she misheard lyrics and sang them.

> *Our hearts are just machinery*
> *Our hearts are just machinery*
> *Our hearts are just machinery*

She had wanted to tell her daughter the cookstove story again. She would have told it and heard her father. She had wanted to do so many things with her daughter before Nimue's silvery thread was cut short.

When Nimue died, Manon fell from the sky and crashed into a million tiny little pieces, which over the years she had been sweeping up. She was slowly regaining her shape, four years later, by medication and sewing and time.

"Her system is doing a second pass" was what Myra Kelley said. "Give her a bit, she's coming along."

The night of the Book Burner, Manon again found herself in a skiff on the water. Naught on a boat at night but noises and the endless sky. She was close to the shore; she could see the fires of the party on the beach. She wondered, but only fleetingly, how many of her creative writing assignments were burning up in the fires.

She searched for her daughter in the dark ripples but saw nothing.

This night Jason had been restless. He went to the sea.

When he came upon his wife in the water they looked at each other for a long time. Jason remembered the smell of her hair and Manon remembered how good his arms felt.

Manon's boat jerked liked it had been bumped by something.

Jason scrambled to toss her the rope and reel her in.

When he pulled her onto the boat it was a long time before he spoke.

"I really fucking miss you, Manon."

She didn't move. She let him speak. The tears poured out of her silently, splayed, mixed with the seawater sloshing on deck. *We each cry an ocean*, she thought.

"She died—"

He broke.

They sobbed together, their grief an invisible border wall.

"She died in your arms. I'm sorry you had to experience that alone. How you screamed." He closed his eyes against the memory.

"I can't explain why I did what I did. I just felt I was supposed to do it, give her body to the mermaid."

He rubbed the wet out of his eyes hard. "I want to believe you." His hands pulsed to hold her, his heartbeat seeking out hers.

"I know. I want to believe me too." She sighed and

momentarily dumped the weight of her grief, the rime on her boat, on Jason's deck.

He would have kissed her then, taken her into his arms and found her lips, to pour in the love he still felt and see if she still tasted like apples and rain. But the boat rocked and split them farther apart bow to stern, and they both looked to the waves.

Two mermaids, one black as obsidian, with silver scales that traveled down her back and rounded her hips like the curves of a violin, the other, kelp green with eyes that shone in the starlight and lips that pouted, swam around the *Pearl*, circling like sharks.

Read in the Red Brocaded Book

"*D*id Captain Burrbank really have a baby with the Mermaid?"

Leo was at Myra's kitchen table, eating. Although he had attended high school parties since he was eleven, he had no interest in the Book Burner that night.

"Ayuh. That's what they say."

Myra was hard-boiling eggs. She normally did a dozen a week for sandwiches and breakfast and such, but each of the last eight weeks or so she had been hard-boiling three dozen.

It did her good to see the boy eating, his bruises all healed up, and looking less skinny.

"But he had a baby with the Piratebird too, right?"

"Ayuh." Myra gave one of the eggs to Dog, who ate it in two bites, one to grab it, one to swallow.

"What was her name?"

"Ariadne Burrbank. She wrote in the book, you know. That poem you like to sing."

"'Until the Moon, Only Then'? She wrote that poem? Cool. Didn't the Piratebird burn Burrbank's house down?"

"Yes, but only because she had to. It was like a beacon. To warn the town and those in the forests."

"Warn them about what, Miss Myra? The mermaids?"

Myra didn't say anything. Leo sighed. Myra relented, something that was happening easier and more and more lately, and began to tell Leo the story while chopping eggs for egg salad.

"One autumn, a year before Torch Night, the mermaid Nimuë came to visit Captain Ichabod alone on the Lone Dock. She brought him their newborn child to be seen once and once only."

They say Ichabod saw the newborn baby, a beautiful wet wiggling baby the color of peaches, fists clenched and cooing. His little bulging belly was ringed by scales adorned by maroon, brown, and yellow stripes that extended into a tail with the spindly fins of a lion fish.

A male, she called him Tristolde, Myra explained, Leo riveted. She let the Captain hold him, his merchild, but once

Burrbank held his son, he could not bear to return him to the great ocean dark.

So Burrbank took the child.

She said that in order to be able to return to his merrow form, for the first full moon cycle of his life the baby was never to touch the sand.

"Did he? Did the baby touch the sand, Miss Myra?"

"Don't talk with your mouth full, especially that full, you might choke, boy. Ayuh, he did. No one knows if it was by accident or on purpose, but Burrbank let his child touch the sand, and his tail split and settled into legs. And he could never return to the ocean to his mother."

Myra dropped an egg. Dog ate it, shell and all.

"That was the Third and final Betrayal. She cursed the town after that," Leo said, incredulously, knowing nothing of the devotion of mothers. "Off of the Lone Docks."

"Off the first Lone Dock."

Fishermen would tell you equally that it was unlucky to dock your boat under a dawn-pink sky at the Lone Dock and also that all superstition was horseshit.

Leo had read in the red brocaded book that when Burrbank took the child, Nimuë disappeared into the dark, and with her went the bounty; nets were only changing the water, coming up empty over and over. A moon cycle later, on Torch Night, when Nimuë came to Mackerel Sky to battle, the sea rose as tall as the cliffs of the Aerie. The Piratebird lit Burrbank's house on fire to alert the land of the danger in the ocean, and up and down the New England coastline bonfires were lit in warning. They say there was still a torch somewhere on High Cliffs, but Leo had never seen it.

Nimuë the Mermaid, framed by the blackest of waves, her breasts a marble bust on the prow, her hair extended in black and indigo tendrils that melded into the water, held the ocean in wait with her hands. Her eyes were cobalt blue, wide whirlpools, rimmed with red. The rain came down and the gales whipped up the water, and the ocean threatened to swallow Mackerel Sky whole.

Then she and her mermaids began to sing, and every man in the town walked toward the sea.

When Nimuë brought the drowning waves and turned the seas into the drowning plains, Burrbank raced the length of the Lone Dock, his heels clapping on the planks, carrying Tristolde. The rain fell in droplets around them, the men walking deeper in the water, the waves crashing on the shore. Tristolde was crying, and for that alone Nimuë held the seas and had the sirens stop singing. The men woke up from their enchanted reveries wherever they were in the sea, but not before the first three had drowned, lured to their death by siren song.

When Nimuë saw her son up close, she could not contain her anguish, for in the rosy hue of the babe's skin she saw the golden glow of earth, intangible; Tristolde could not change back to a merrow and return with his mother. He had touched the sand. He would be a child of the land, the final betrayal.

She screeched to the moon, the rain beating her breast.

The account in the big red book ended there, but the stories told fireside and hearthside continued on. Some said Nimuë settled when she saw the baby, that she would not destroy her son's new home with him in it, but others maintained that a mermaid felt differently toward a land-child. Some said she saw naught but Burrbank. Some said she slapped him when she met him at the Lone Dock; others described a kiss—a wave carrying her up and she kissing him just as the Piratebird came down the Aerie brandishing a sword, face plastered with rain.

Then the sea, under Nimuë's command, vomited up her dead merman brother, his body mangled and strangled in a fishing net.

And the town would answer for its crimes.

Many in Mackerel Sky shared stories of how their ancestors were heroes, how they battled the mermaids with torches and fire arrows, how they died that night. The Feathers of the Piratebird and Burrbank's crew—the Terror, the Man with the Monkey, the Tattooed Twins—were Mackerel Sky's strongest battalion, somehow immune to the mermaids' song, and they dragged many an enchanted sailor from the brink of death in the drink. The Piratebird and her priestess lover, Burning Owl, fought the mermaids from the shallows to the dock's end until the dark night glowed with the warm break of day.

In the end, eight men went into the sea.

"Life's just one fucking tragedy after another," said Myra.

Dog started barking up a frenzy, interrupting Myra's storytelling.

Poppy Beale, Leo's mother, walked up the crooked driveway, bowlegged on skinny legs in too-short shorts, cranking a butt and picking her teeth. Her eyeliner was thick and eyes bloodshot, furtive. She was high on something; she walked liked she was rocking on the waves and twitched like she was being pinched by an invisible entourage.

"You wrecked a fucking car?" Months and months too late. She had forgotten. She tossed the unfinished cigarette and left it smoking on the ground while she lit another. "What the fuck is wrong with you?"

Leo wanted to gesture to all of her, but he didn't. He came out onto the porch. Myra Kelley, who herself had buried two babies, was always stunned to meet a mother who wasn't a mother. In this way, Poppy Beale was like a derelict cargo ship, empty once she was at port and had delivered. Myra followed behind Leo, grabbed her broom, and then stepped in front of him to speak.

"He's working off his debt. We have a gentleman's agreement. He's paying his due."

"Really? Any money he makes belongs to me, you old bitch."

"Jesus Christ, Mom." Leo felt sick. He didn't want Mrs. Myra to be treated like this, to see his mother like this, tweaking. She kept grinding her jaw and swatting at flies that didn't exist.

"Poppy, I think you best be on your way." Myra had her broom; Dog sat at her heels and growled, adding a low bass rumble to underscore her words. Leo thought he saw a flash of light near her wrists, but then it disappeared.

"You don't say shit to me about my kid, you stupid hag. You been spending too much time over here, brat. I need you back at the trailer; you got shit to do." Leo's stomach turned thinking about the close, sweaty, smoky air of that home, the overflowing ashtrays and molding food, the sloppy noises at night. He liked Myra's house; there was always electricity and food and no drugs or bruises or black eyes. He liked not worrying about anyone coming into his bedroom except Dog.

Myra switched the broom into her left hand.

"I'm going to say this again. I think it's time you be leaving my property, Poppy, or I'll ring the sheriff. He won't like being called out here on a Friday night."

Poppy's face contorted and spittle flew: "I bet you'd like that, wouldn't you, bitch! I tell you what, this is done after this weekend! I've got a big weekend that isn't going to get screwed up by you, but when I come back you better believe you are fucking coming home, Leo—no more hanging at Myra's; she ain't your family! You'll do as I say—*I am your fucking mother!*"

Poppy tripped over herself and a chicken storming off on the Paths, another burning cigarette in her wake.

The silence stretched long after she was gone until Dog

whined a bit, his jowls resting on his paws. Leo quietly picked up the cigarette butts from Myra's driveway.

"Sometimes those chickens come in handy," Myra said, and Leo snorted, once, twice, and then burst out laughing.

"Bernie was right sometimes, God rest his soul." She said it and then saw that Leo was crying quietly, trying to hide his face. She put a hand on his shoulder and drew him into a hug when the sobs crested and broke. "Boy," she said, "you stay as long as you like. Normally I'd tell a child to listen to his mother, but that woman doesn't have a brain in her fucking head."

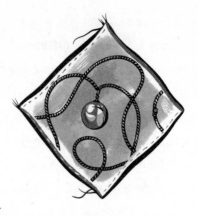

The Gift of the Green Pearl

*D*errick Stowe didn't have to grow up in the Townsend house on the crap end of Beacon Street to recognize the rage in Jared Townsend's bloodshot eyes, nor did he need to see him sock out two of his baby brother Ricky's teeth to know the twins were coming for him. Instinct kicked in, the need to survive, and he became feral, desperate, though still determined to lead them away from Ricky, who was now picking up his teeth from the ground of Mermaid's Mouth.

"Hey, assholes! He says he learned how to kiss boys by

watching you two!" The chum was tossed and Derrick turned and ran, hoping the sharks would follow.

Derrick and his mother used to visit Myra and Bernie Kelley; Myra let Millicent read from the famous red brocaded book and take notes for her research before she drowned. Bernie would smoke his pipe and feed the chickens and tell a much younger Derrick stories about the war while Derrick played with dump trucks until the old man nodded off in the rocking chair on the porch.

"I remember running the beach in Normandy, with my two good pals, Nate and Jimmy Jr.," Bernie told him once. "The bullets made the sand explode; my goggles got so scratched up they were no good after that. I saw a dune and turned to tell the boys to take cover. They were facedown in the sand."

Derrick remembered this story as his feet pounded the sand of Crescent Beach, his breath in rhythm, blood rushing to his ears. *Don't end up facedown in the sand like Nate and Jimmy Jr.*, he thought, over and over. He ran from the Book Burner bonfires into the dark.

The Townsend twins followed, the alcohol and speed pills the stick and gas to their car.

Back at Derrick's house, Stéphane slept in the armchair next to the fireplace, open book on his belly and Duke at his feet. Suddenly, Duke got up and began whining at the door, then scratching, then barking, enough of a din to rouse a sleeping fisherman. Blade raced to the door, alert for intruders, but he opened the door to no one.

Duke bolted out into the night toward the fires.

Ricky gingerly supported his temple, nursing a killer headache and a throbbing mouth, the blood pumping out in warm rivulets with every heartbeat. Jared had knocked out two teeth in Ricky's mouth on the left and split his lip open wide, a solid right hook. Jared and Colby and Ricky all learned how to fight and drink from their father, but as they grew up Ricky found refuge in books, while his brothers found it in OxyContin and anger.

Thus the cursed cycle continued in the Townsend family.

Ricky was able to find his teeth because the pearl in the necklace Derrick had given him was glowing bright green like it was lit from within. Ricky got up and stumbled out of Mermaid's Mouth, his shirt unbuttoned, the glowing lime orb bouncing on his chest, bouncing faster as he picked up pace. He had to get to Derrick; his brothers would kill him.

Don't end up facedown in the sand, Derrick repeated to himself over and over as his running, stumbling feet dug up the sand, *You won't ever get up*.

Derrick might have escaped too: he was faster, more in shape, and smoked rarely. But Derrick's eyes flicked to the water, and he thought he saw a blue, bare-breasted woman burst out of the sea, struggling in a net, and it gave him pause. Then a wave crashed over her and he saw nothing of the sort anymore.

That look was enough to make him stumble, and Jared overtook him, Colby not far behind.

Stéphane had no time to get his jacket and barely enough time to close the door in pursuit of Duke, who took off on one of the Paths toward Crescent Beach. Stéphane was fast, but not as fast as a retriever with a scent, and soon he was just following the sound of the dog's barks, which did not decrease in their intensity.

Ricky did not make it to Derrick in time.

The first hit came from behind, where Jared sacked Derrick to the ground, and then kicked him in the kidney and ribs in an upward blow. Derrick felt a pop and a bright pain in his side but managed to elbow Jared and break his nose, which allowed him room to get out from under the other boy. But there Colby stood ready to pave his twin's path of destruction, and he clocked Derrick in the jaw. They didn't call Derrick Rembrandt for nothing—mouth bleeding, he pulled back and punched Colby in the face with his pitching gun, and the kid went down to the ground, but then he spat the blood out of his mouth and rose again. Jared socked Derrick in the stomach and Derrick fell to his knees, after which the brothers descended on him like the dark wave of a tsunami and began kicking him and punching him in the head.

They stopped only because they heard an alien screech, a sound that pierced the air and stung. They looked around, confused, bleary-eyed, but the sound did not repeat, and they were drunk enough to wonder if they imagined it.

Then they noticed that Derrick had stopped fighting back.

"That's what faggots are good for," Jared said and spat. "Bleeding."

Then they ran.

They were gone when Ricky arrived under the light of the moon. Derrick was a bloody, pulpy mess. He was barely breathing. Blood bubbled out of his mouth and nose. Ricky cried over him, the tears and snot dribbling over Derrick as he rolled him over and saw his swollen face and bruised ribs in the green light of the necklace.

"Derrick? Coffee Bean? Come on, wake up!" Ricky cried, again and again. Derrick didn't answer. Ricky dialed 911—the ambulance would take too long to arrive, but he didn't know what else to do.

Stéphane had heard the strange screech as he ran to the beach. It was hurting, desperate, a plea. A call for help. Blade had heard a yell like that before, but he couldn't remember where or when. He saw Duke farther down the beach and ran.

He came upon Ricky, his arms wrapped around Derrick, rocking, repeating his name like a mantra. Duke whined and howled, then cocked his head toward the ocean.

A single hand, ensnared by a fishing net, reached up out of the black waters and then was sucked back down.

Only Duke saw.

"Derrick? What? Derrick! Mon fils— What the hell!" Blade dove down to the ground and ran his hands along the wounds on his son's body, checked his breathing. "What happened, Ricky? Did you call nine-one-one?"

Ricky nodded, then faded to Stéphane's periphery as Stéphane focused on his son struggling to breathe.

Then another inhuman howl from the water slit the sky.

Ricky and Blade turned to the sea, where a violet mermaid thrashed violently in the drink. She was struggling with a large net that the waves kept dragging to the shore. In the net was another mermaid, cerulean, trapped, desperate. Stéphane looked between the struggling mermaids and his bloodied son. The mermaid screamed again, a mournful wail, the lonely call of a whale.

Ricky began crying. "You have to save her. I'll stay with Derrick. We can't do anything but wait."

Stéphane shook his head vehemently. He would not leave his son.

The mermaid bellowed, whimpered, begged. The sound was agonizing.

"Please," Ricky pleaded. "I would, but I can't swim."

Stéphane remembered the seagull limping around the boatyard, avoiding trucks and trailers and alley cats. Stéphane remembered thinking it was a matter of time before the bird was roadkill. So he wrapped it in a towel and learned that day that birds could be soothed by being swaddled, for Plum fell asleep in the split leather seat of the truck.

"Okay," Stéphane agreed, kissing his boy and patting Ricky on the shoulder. "Stay with him! I'll come back." Stéphane unsheathed a knife with a bone handle from his belt and ran into the water. Sharp and shiny in the starlight, the blade had been in his family for generations. He went to cut the net, and the purple mermaid hissed and flashed teeth like an angler fish.

"You best back off," Blade warned the creature, flashing his knife, and she shrunk back a little bit but hovered close by, the spiky dorsal fins on her tail splayed in warning. Blade set to the net and scuttled about it like a crab, his fingers and the knife speedily slicing and slipping the knots and netting off the writhing mermaid. The other mermaid, her hair glinting silver and nacre under the moon, opened black eyes wide, swam a bit back, wary and watchful. Stéphane was up to his waist, the waves cresting over him, waiting for the ambulance for his dying boy, but he cut the cerulean mermaid free and made quick work of it. Once out, she slipped under the sea, sluicing through the current, joyful to swim freely again.

Stéphane returned immediately to his son and held him like a baby for the first time since he was a baby. Derrick coughed once, took a big, shaky, rattling breath, and then stopped breathing.

The wail that Stéphane's body expelled was ancient, devastated. It caught the attention of the amethystine mermaid who had called for help. She watched the flurry of human activity at the end of the beach, her head bobbing above the waves. She swam slowly, tentatively, to the boundary of the water and land and pulled herself to lie at the edge of the beach, the waves crashing on her. Her tail unfurled like petals, the scales reflecting the night light as prisms. She pushed herself up, a cobra, and slithered onto the shore. Once completely on the sand, her body began shuddering and she pulled into herself like a snail.

Stéphane and Ricky watched her, both guarding Derrick's limp body.

Suddenly the mermaid stood and her scales fell away like dry sand and disintegrated into bright dust, revealing two human legs. She walked on these legs toward the trio, Derrick now cradled protectively in Blade's arms, Ricky standing behind, his eyes wide and brimming.

The woman was nude. She was breathtakingly beautiful. She was mesmerizing, her body transforming from its plum purple hue to a human peach tone. She looked at both Ricky and Blade like they were experiments, specimens to examine, but then she turned to Derrick and her lips parted in shock. She lowered to her knees. Blade watched her like a lion, his hand on the bone handle of his knife. She looked to him first, examined his eyes for a long time, and then very gently placed her hand on the hand that held the hilt of his blade, and she held his eyes and hand until she saw what she needed to see: a tiny bit of trust.

She then moved her hands in front of her face, her third eye, middle fingers and palms touching like she was cradling the moon. After a whisper in a language that sounded like the secrets offered by seashells, she placed her hand on Derrick's still chest, and then lower to his bruised ribs. She looked at Stéphane then, a silent request of approval, and he nodded, so she cupped her hand and grabbed Derrick's side forcefully.

A wave crashed. A star fell.

And Derrick Stowe sputtered and started, and vomited up blood.

He was breathing.

Ambulance sirens crescendoed in the background.

He was alive.

Blade clasped her hand and repeated a rosary of gratitude. Ricky did as well, but her head cocked when she laid eyes on his pearl necklace, still emanating its emerald light. She stood, jolted, and backed up. She reached for the necklace for a moment, but then snapped her hand away.

Ricky didn't think twice. He pulled the leather thong over his head and offered it to her, a small price for what he had received. He would have given her anything. She wouldn't take it until Ricky placed it over her head, but then she smiled at him and placed her hand on his cheek, and though Ricky considered himself almost 100 percent gay on the Kinsey scale, in that moment, when her wet eyes held his, he understood why sailors leapt from their decks for the deep. She cocked her head and her eyes beckoned. In a daze, like moving through water, Ricky reached for her, but Blade slapped the boy's hand back.

Then the mermaid swam away, for the world was coming.

Ricky didn't know how true that would remain in the wash, but he took it for the moment it was.

When Derrick was loaded up on the ambulance, Blade

blinked and inhaled deeply, relieved, a temporary eye in this new storm. He looked at Ricky then through glassy eyes and said, "I'm glad you were there, Ricky."

That morning, before dawn and at the end of night, when the last of the Book Burner's revelers had been cleared out by cops and ambulances, Ricky snuck into his childhood home and took some clothes, his meager summer work savings, his phone and charger, and his favorite fox stuffed animal. The stale cigarettes and beatings clinging to him, his future wide open, Ricky left forever that place where the rotting Christmas Pig lorded over its hoard, and began walking away, walking on Beacon Street toward the ocean, toward the lighthouse, and didn't look back.

The Cavernous Quiet

Unconscious, in his coma, Derrick broke into the abyss through its surface like Alice through the looking glass. Two halves of his whole touched through fingertips where the ocean met a mackerel sky. He plunged into the gradient of gray and swam down to the black-ink depths. He was naked and unafraid and thankful for the cavernous quiet when no one could bother him and he could think.

He swam deeper and deeper. The water was warm and fathomless and his, all his to explore.

In the water, over and over, he saw his mother.

A wall of water beside him shimmered and he was looking into a mirror he knew well, his mother's oval vanity with the tarnished corner and the haphazard jazz band of vintage colored glass bottles. He was looking at himself, but from when he was much younger, around five, with awkwardly, reverently smeared lipstick over his lips and chin. His mother came behind him, chin on his shoulder. She cleaned up where he had missed and filled in what was missing. His lips were red and perfect.

"Beautiful. Just as you are." She kissed him; he felt full.

His father's brow farther away came into focus in the mirror. He too looked younger, less weathered. His mother and his father locked eyes. Gently, warmly, patiently, she smiled at him, and he unsurely smiled back.

"How do I tell him?" Derrick asked the reflection in the mirror.

"He already knows," she replied.

They dissolved into bubbles and another panel of water rippled, and in it he saw himself on the beach pitching to his dad, puppy Duke chasing balls, his mother swimming effortlessly in the waves. The sky was a repeating time-lapse film sunrise to sunrise, the colors blooming apricot and smoke and pink, and then the sun traveling its chariot arc and melting into ruby and embers and then the black night, the stars falling into stardust. He pitched, the smart *thwack* of the ball hitting the mitt getting stronger, the dog and the boy growing bigger and older over days and months and years. He slung his slider, and the world tilted on its axis, and he was upside down, falling, falling, and he landed on an oarless skiff in the middle of the ocean.

The entire sea was still.

Sunrise had just broken, the yolk orb peeking out from under the lowest cloud. A lone humpback breached. Derrick thought he could hear it singing. The sun rose higher and shone behind a cloud. The water—*still still*—was a creamy blue.

Then the waves began to beat a rhythm, the ocean returning to her turbulent self.

The main was full of mermaids.

He saw them in all ways. He saw them as obsidian beacons in milk mist, lounging on rocks like sculptures and statues, lighthouses of longing. He saw them as a school of tiger sharks, frenzied, ferocious. He saw them as unforgettable, haunting dreams, curves and scales that had lured sailors from the safety of their ships into the depths for all of time. They swam to him, swam away from him, men and women, their tails and bodies colors he knew well and colors he had never seen before. They beckoned to him, thrashing, threshing.

He stood and stripped in the sun, dove off the boat, off the world, and followed them into the water and joined their school, swirling and twirling down into the dark.

And then suddenly his mother appeared beside him, racing him, her tail long strong, a gradient of cobalt to onyx, a long fin at the end like a thresher shark.

His mother, the mermaid. Here, in the underworld reality of his subconscious, the thought settled comfortably into absolute truth. Of course his mother was a mermaid. He flipped backward in the file cabinet in his mind and found a skeleton memory fleshing itself out: his mother, pale, wan, gratefully drinking a cup of tea Myra Kelley offered while he played with a yellow truck under Bernie's knees on the front porch with all the singing wind chimes, Myra watching as his mother poured water on her legs, as they sprouted dark blue scales that bloomed all over until they covered her up to her waist like drops of rain pooling together to cover a surface. He saw the scales looked desiccated, weathered, faded, and when Myra encouraged his mother to drink some tea, the scales brightened, sparkled. Myra Kelley nodded, encouraged at the results.

He had the memory filed differently: he and Mr. Bernie were talking about what it might be like to own chickens and the war until Mr. Bernie dozed off and Derrick went to bulldoze Queen Anne's lace in the yard . . . but that was not entirely correct, because there was his truck abandoned in the grasses, Mr. Bernie dozing in the rocker, and here he was listening at the door.

"I cannot give it to him. I have tried, but once a mermaid's pearl leaves the sea it must travel its own route back to the ocean. It is not for me to give it to him, but I am able to give it to you, so you must take it, Lorelei. My time here is ending. The pearl has to leave me so it can somehow get to my son."

Young Derrick, eavesdropping in the dream, heard what sounded like the heavy snap of rigging, and the lockbox door on Myra's Christmas cabinet cracked open.

"Land sakes," mused Myra Kelley. She nodded then, like she was in agreement with the cabinet, and reached an open hand to Millicent. Millie plucked the green stone that was embedded in her favorite journal. She set it into a leather strap necklace and held it out to Myra.

"There will come a time when in your heart, you will know to give it to him. I can't tell you when: Mermaid pearls travel the land as they wish. They stay and get attached to some humans, make them powerful, magical. I cannot tell you when to give it to him, but you will know. It must touch his skin before it returns to the sea; then he will be accepted into my kin. The pearl told me it would be safe with you, that its kindred have been safe with you before."

Myra took the necklace and put it in a velvet pouch, which she tucked into Burrbank's coffer, closed the safe, and locked it.

Derrick swam away from the memory, back into the dark, his mother swimming beside him. He matched her pace and was shocked to find himself launched forward, propelled, and he looked back over his shoulder and saw that his legs had vanished, replaced by his own hyacinthine tail with its own long thresher fin.

"I knew you couldn't have drowned, Mom," he told her. "You were always such a good swimmer."

She smiled and shot off, leaving him in a wake of bubbles that surrounded him like a cage of pearls.

The bubbles changed into words from his poetry as they passed him.

It was blissful
When I called you yesterday
And you came through, came up
Placed yourself near my womb,
Guarded it like a sphinx
And said you could end here
It would be blissful
To die like this
Coiling and winding caduceus
I was all open
And transformed
You are a muse
I am only listening, Love

Derrick stopped swimming for a moment then, suspended in a dark world of gray. He thought of Ricky, warm flashes of memory. Ricky cheering at a game, Ricky glancing at him while passing out papers in Mrs. Perle's class, Ricky smoking a cigarette, his head on Derrick's stomach, listening to his boyfriend's stabs at poetry.

Only then, the water extending forever all around him, did

Derrick remember he was actually human, not a mermaid, and that no human could breathe underwater.

He opened his mouth and water rushed in.

His scream was muffled, almost silent, and no one heard, not even his father, who was sitting right next to him in the hospital in the bland mauve bedside chair, a book open and turned over on his thigh, an empty paper coffee cup on the windowsill beside him. Stéphane couldn't sleep well at home; he had become too used to the sounds of the machines that helped his child breathe; at home he woke in the night and didn't hear them and thought Derrick was dead. So he drove to the hospital and preferred to rest sitting upright in the dull chair, where the beat of the heart monitor lulled him to sleep. His neck hurt in the mornings and the coffee was bad, but the nurses were kind and brought him blankets, and his son was still breathing, if nothing else.

Ricky Townsend had also been in the hospital almost every day. He read Derrick poems by Langston Hughes, ate too much Jell-O, and watched Red Sox games on the room's TV. He relayed the baseball stats of the home team, but the news wasn't good, the Mackerel Sky Tritons were getting trounced without their star pitcher. Derrick's jersey—Jackie Robinson's 42—was hung on the right field chain-link fence every game. People laid flowers against the fence outside of the field, which Ricky later brought to the hospital. There got to be so many that he started to give them away, to nurses, mothers of players, to Gladys, Beatrix, and Agathe-Alice. He put them on Derrick's mother's gravestone.

Stéphane knew that Ricky and Derrick were friends, but he wondered when Ricky and Derrick had become such close friends. But one day, when Stéphane came upon Ricky adjusting Derrick's pillow, repeating the action three times before he was satisfied, he saw Ricky, ever so gently, brush a bit of spittle off his son's lip and let his fingertips rest against his boyfriend's warm skin for the briefest of moments, enough of a moment for the father to see and realize what had been kept secret.

And Stéphane's heart broke because his boy hadn't felt he could share his happiness with him.

That night while they watched a ball game Blade offered Ricky a blanket. Ricky shared his Jell-O. Ricky didn't understand what, but somehow something had changed and he no longer felt that his presence was a confusion but was rather a welcomed expectation.

Derrick's face was less swollen, but still looked like a pink-and-purple smashed dinner plate. He had swelling in his brain and seven broken bones, including his collarbone, nose, cheekbone, and four ribs, which, according to the doctors, should have killed him the night of the Book Burner. The broken ribs should have punctured his lung, leaving Derrick to drown in his own blood. One doctor kept examining the X-rays and scans and concluded it *had* been punctured but had somehow, someway, miraculously healed. He couldn't explain it.

Blade was not about to explain mermaids, to the doctors or himself, not until his only child was conscious, anyway; he also found most folk not open to that sort of thing, so he shrugged his shoulders, shut his mouth about mermaids, and called Derrick's healed lung injury an act of God.

The prognosis was time, many machines, and hope.

Out the hospital window Stéphane saw the hazy colored glows of fireworks. It was the Fourth of July.

He had been holding his hospital vigil for two full weeks.

Ghost Gear

*T*hey say bodies floated in the water off the Lone Dock that morning in 1721. The sunrise after Torch Night was broken, the clouds covering the sky like scales on fish flesh, filtering the sunlight, breaking it into beacons spotlighting the dead.

The newly founded town of Mackerel Sky was small, but it was fierce and scrappy. Though a settlement of but twenty or so buildings at that point, it was rooted in the earth and a beloved home to all who lived there. Under the command of

Burrbank and his crew, beside the Wabanaki and the Feathers of the Piratebird, the residents fought valiantly against the onslaught of mermaids and ocean on Torch Night. The Piratebird set Burrbank's house ablaze, both a fiery call to arms and a mortal warning for the mermaids born terrified of fire. The Feathers tore lit boards off the house and stabbed them deep into Crescent Beach, a boundary of jagged, burning teeth. Some townsfolk died in the ocean wrenching their loved ones away from the waves and the mermaids' song, or the mermaids themselves, who had snapped on the men in the water like crocodiles and dragged them to the bottom. The Feathers of the Piratebird fought with their burning boards and bows and fire arrows. The town fought with kitchen knives and pitchforks and bonfires. The mermaids fought with whalebone spears and shark-tooth maces and the ocean itself and their siren song, its dulcet melody the deadliest of lures. They say that that night the Feathers of the Piratebird countered with their own land magic, learned from the Wabanaki and Burning Owl, but the only record of such beyond myth was said to be in the big red book, and Myra Kelley was mum.

Three truths rose with the shattered sunlight that day: Tristolde Alain Burrbank would remain a child of the land, the mermaids were gone from the town, never to return as before, and in their wake they left a curse, a storm cloud that settled angrily over Mackerel Sky indefinitely.

The morning of the broken sunrise a new graveyard was

built at the end of the town, far from the ocean. A statue—a virgin on the rocks facing due east, her clothes blowing off in the wind, one hand reaching to the main, mid-step toward the cliff—stood in the cemetery in tribute to all those lost, those with graves at sea, unvisitable resting places. They erected eight stones that day, some cenotaphs, some gravestones, for some of the bodies from Torch Night washed up on the shore, some disappeared forever, lost to the vast unmarked tomb of the sea.

But that would not be the end of it.

The next winter was the most brutal on record in Mackerel Sky. The blizzards and illness decimated the survivors of Torch Night and took another nine. In the red book it said that those who suffered from the affliction of the winter lung of 1721 coughed like they were drowning, and save for winters of war the winter of 1721 was one of the worst on record. Ultimately the town paid the mermaids' losses with twenty-one lives that year: eight when the mermaids attacked, nine during January and February, one drowning in spring, and three drownings in summer.

In the decade that followed, all of Burrbank's crew left Mackerel Sky and returned to a life on the sea, all save one: his copain de vie, Stéphane's ancestor Alain, the Terror in the Night. Burrbank and Alain had a knack for saving each other's skins and grieved life's griefs together. Alain grew to Mackerel Sky like a great pine, driving roots deep, seeking water from the Acadians and the Wabanaki. His tomb, erected many,

many years later, set under a hill at the end of the cemetery, was surrounded by a lush brushstroke of wildflowers spring to fall, a favorite spot of high schoolers for senior photos.

Ever since the morning of the broken sunrise, the sea thenceforth claimed more inhabitants of Mackerel Sky than most towns on the Maine coast, victims like one of the Tattooed Twins, like Jason's twenty-two-year-old brother, Vincent, like little Nimue Perle.

The morning of the Mermaid Festival, four years after her daughter died, Manon walked up the crooked drive to Myra Kelley's front porch, hands in her pockets, hair flowing around her cheekbones. She had stopped by Myra Kelley's for a steadying coffee this morning of all mornings. She had entered her quilt into the auction but would not stick around the downtown busy with tourists and locals to see how it fared. When she and Jason had Nimue, they would have been on a boat by now, watching the lobster-boat races with a soda in one hand and a crabmeat sandwich in the other, her child on her lap. She looked at the ocean, sparkling, inviting. She looked at her child's tomb.

She hadn't been back on the water since Jason rescued her the night of the Book Burner, the night they saw the two mermaids circle the *Pearl* then sharply swim for the seaboard, drawn by a distinct virescent lucent orb, some jade firefly upon the shore. Jason gunned his engine all the way back to the wharf, and by the time they got to the Crescent the ambulance had already taken Derrick Stowe to the hospital, and the truth of what happened was already becoming stretched and colored and exaggerated, though the consensus was that there might have been another mermaid sighting and that Derrick Stowe might not live through the night thanks to the good-for-nothing Townsend twins. When Jason looked back for Manon, he saw nothing but the crowd; she had returned to haunt the Lone Docks.

When she had Nimue, the morning of the Mermaid Festival she and Jason would be looking forward to a picnic out on Iledest Island, but she had been avoiding him since the night of the Book Burner, avoiding most people. The town was once again abuzz with the topic of mermaids; this time of year Manon preferred to be out of town the most, away from tourists discovering her daughter's story as an anecdote in a travel guide, away from locals pointing and whispering factoids about Nimue's coffin being empty.

Iledest Island was directly east of Mackerel Sky and founded by some lost adventurous Acadians. Iledest was French, and literally meant East Island, or Island of the East, but most residents of Mackerel Sky did not speak French and so the redundancy of the word *island* in the moniker Iledest Island was lost. The island was a favorite of locals for camping and bonfires and clambakes. Manon had not been there since she carried her daughter across its sands.

When Manon arrived at Myra's front porch, Jason opened the door holding a cup of coffee. They stood still for a long time, just breathing, holding the moment in their eyes. Manon was keenly aware of the warmth emanating from Jason's body, and how easy it would be to settle hers on his in an embrace and feel her muscle tension release filament by filament. Jason leaned forward the tiniest bit, lost in her as he had always been, then stepped back, ever so slightly, and held the door open wider, gesturing once with his coffee in welcome.

Manon entered Myra's kitchen, and encountered Leo at the table eating hard-boiled eggs with butter and white toast, Dog catching scraps at his feet.

"Hi, Mrs. Perle!" he said enthusiastically, his mouth full of egg.

"Don't speak with your mouth full, boy; we only like one kind of seafood here," Myra ordered.

Leo nodded and mumbled apologies. Manon waved.

"Coffee's hot. Another cup, Jason?" Myra offered, though Jason had not taken his eyes off of Manon. He nodded, snapped out of his reverie, and pulled out a chair for her.

They sat at the table with Leo and their coffees—Jason's with cream and sugar, Manon pouring in the cream, Myra's decaf, black.

"So, lots of mermaid activity as of late, Jason tells me," said Myra after a sip, after a beat.

Leo dropped his fork, flabbergasted. He stopped chewing so he wouldn't miss a sound. Jason looked at Manon with wet eyes as if he would break.

"I told Myra you were right. That I didn't believe you," said Jason. "I told her that we saw two back in June, off the boat, the night of the Book Burner, when Blade's boy got beaten up." Manon nodded, stirring in her cream.

Myra sighed. "Poor babe. Still in a coma. Bless his little heart." She had been praying every night for Derrick, and Leo.

"Going on seven weeks. My sternman's sister works at the hospital," said Jason, almost finished with his second coffee already.

The table was collectively silent, the weight of the tragedy silencing them.

"I saw a mermaid," offered Leo, hesitantly.

"Yeah? Welcome to the club, kid," Jason responded.

Leo sat straighter and secretly smiled into his eggs. When he looked up, Jason was again staring at Manon. She cupped her coffee and watched the steam.

Manon remained silent. Leo looked at Myra, expectant. She released an audible sigh.

"I've seen more mermaids than I care to remember. Nuisance, mostly, the lot of them. But honestly, it's the sea witches you really need to look out for. They are one of the real dangers in the ocean. Top-off?" She got up from the table and grabbed the coffee pot. "You two going in town for the festivities?"

Manon shook her head before the question was even finished. "No, not this year. Too many tourists." *Too many memories.* "You?"

"Up to Leo here."

Leo perked up at his name and his options. He absolutely

loved the Mermaid Festival. He usually went alone and broke, but it was always an opportunity to get out of a trailer full of his mother's wasted friends. His hopeful smile at Myra filled her heart.

"We're going, then. But only two treats—I don't want you coming back here with a stomachache."

"Two? *Two?*" Two treats was double: one treat plus one treat was more treats than Leo had ever gotten any year at the Mermaid Festival. Leo jumped from his chair and hugged Myra then, who was squishy and smelled like Bernie's soap and chuckled deep in her belly when he leaned in.

"Can we go soon? I want fried dough wicked bad."

"Ayuh. Make your bed first."

"Miss Myra, can't I do it after?" he whined, the words long and forced.

"Leo, don't let every day be a new adventure in excuses."

As he always did, Dog went with him.

Jason still had not stopped looking at Manon, her sprinkling of freckles, her long, almost elfish ears, her piano fingers wrapped around the warm mug.

"Come with me," he pleaded suddenly, not realizing where he wanted to go with her until he finished the question. He would have gone anywhere with her, escaped to anywhere with her where they could run from the world, but today there was only one place he wanted to go with her. "Come with me, to Iledest."

Manon looked up at him then, and saw the understanding, the present, the light in his eyes. She thought of the sunrise this morning, when once again the Three Bats surprised her, awake, stitching in their rocking chairs, overseeing the harbor. When she asked them why they were up so early, Gladys answered, "Goddamned mermaids."

"That nice husband of yours coming around today?" asked Beatrix, pulling the thread through to punctuate the words *husband* and *today*.

When Manon shook her head, Gladys snorted. "That's a fucking shame."

"Ayuh," concluded Agathe-Alice.

Manon thought about how lonely her bed had been of late, how she kept waking up to cuddle with someone who was not there. She thought about how Jason looked at her when he saw the mermaids the night of the Book Burner, like coming home, like ghost gear returning to the shore.

"Okay," she offered.

Jason saw the window of opportunity crack open with a sliver of light and immediately took her hand and lifted her to her feet.

On the porch was a picnic basket from Myra Kelley, already packed.

On the boat, Jason watched, enthralled, as Manon came alive, rocking with the water, at peace, the wind in her hair. They sat for a long while in silence, contented by the sharp sea air and the constant, soothing, in utero drone of the engine. When beyond the reach, Manon spoke out loud, to Jason and the wind and the sea:

"Do you know how Myra met Bernie? It was during the war, when she was in high school, during a dance. She was crying with her friends because a boy they had gone to school with had been killed in combat. Bernie gave her a handkerchief. I thought that was beautiful. He wiped her tears away."

The last time either one of them had been to Iledest they had come with their daughter. The island's empty beach and tall pines grew in view. They anchored, rowed in on a skiff, and silently walked on the sand, Myra's picnic basket packed for two between them.

There used to be a child in their arms. She died this day four years ago. They carried their love for her; they carried her memory, carried her ghost.

Where they moored there was a corner of the beach called Pirate's Trove, where the current and the tides washed up haberdashery and ghost gear, lobstering equipment that had come untethered, lost, homeless: how Jason felt until he brought Manon back onto his boat. Residents of Mackerel Sky looked for treasure there, and Nimue's cache was still in her bedroom, covered in dust, untouched. They used to trade some of their treasures with the backyard crows.

"I have to feed the crows again," Manon said to no one in particular. She played with the pearl earring in her pocket.

Manon didn't think she would ever be able to go back to

the island where Nimue ate her last meal, but returning was less jarring than she thought it would be; the memories and the pain were more akin to the buzzing of a mosquito than the wasp nest she feared. It wasn't the place she dreaded, it was the loss that happened there, and the loss had already happened. There was nothing left to be taken.

This time as they walked the beach, she felt Jason steady beside her, like a rock she could break upon, over and over.

He took her hand, and her fingers melted into his.

She and Jason shared lunch on a blanket while the clouds grew heavy. They hadn't expected rain, but the thunderstorm rolled in heedless of their plans and set Jason to seeking shelter for them in Iledest's woods. He found refuge under some tall firs, a rock outcropping, and their blanket. When he returned to Manon, she was standing in the pouring rain while the waves rioted around her.

He took her hand and she turned to him and saw him again, her lighthouse in the storm.

They kissed in the wind and the rain, their embrace as wild as the weather.

Under the blanket on the soft wet forest floor they found each other, and filled themselves with each other, and making love under their makeshift lean-to felt like coming home. Although their house would always be haunted, it was theirs.

Between Gun and Broomstick

"Myra, why is Dog named Dog?"

"That's what he responds to."

They were sitting on the grass waiting for the Mermaid Festival's annual parade.

"Why didn't you name him?"

"I named him accidentally. He came to my house the first night I spent alone after Bernie died. He wouldn't come in and mostly stayed outside for three months. I called him Dog the whole time, and now that's what he answers to."

"Then what?"

"Then he curled up by the fire one night and started farting and snoring, and he hasn't stopped since."

Leo laughed and petted Dog, who was farting and snoring next to them in the grass in the sun. Dog was a good old dog. Myra petted him and said, "Who's my Mr. Big and Handsome Dog?"

"Mr. Big and Handsome Dog?" Leo's eyes widened.

"His full name. I use it when he is being particularly noble or particularly handsome."

That early weekend of August, when the nights were warm and the gardens were red and yellow and riotous, the town celebrated the mermaids with high praise. No matter where one stood in their beliefs regarding the existence of mermaids, for three days in August every resident was not only a mermaid believer but an expert, especially before the tourists. In general Mackerel Sky looked upon tourists like most Maine towns did—as outsiders, a necessary evil, and, during the festival, a much-needed infusion of cash. Mermaid-seeking tourists spilled in and took over every inn and bed-and-breakfast and run-down motel up and down the coast. They ate at the Mermaid's Tail, walked the Lone Docks, laughed at the Mackerel Sky Punch and Judy show, which had been operated by a Smith now for over one hundred years. Tourists typically didn't attend Jason's memorial, a vigil held at sunset the second night of the festival; they wanted the legend of the mermaids, not the reality.

Leo had the best day of his dang life, even though Mrs. Myra said there was a threat of a thunderstorm. He didn't see any clouds, but he didn't care anyway because Mrs. Myra gave him ten whole dollars of his own to spend. First he bought himself fried dough with lots of cinnamon and powdered sugar. He also got one for Mrs. Myra because he didn't want to eat without sharing, but she declined and said it was too sweet for her—and that he should have it! So he had two fried doughs before eleven in the morning. Then the parade came by, the homemade floats pulled by trucks, the marching bands, the clowns, the small car Shriners, the beauty queens in Mustangs and Camaros, the cops and robbers and candy, so, so much candy tossed to the crowd.

Leo had his Tritons baseball cap full of candy by the end. He gave a Tootsie Roll to Myra because that was her favorite, and took some lollipops and a chocolate for himself, and then, because he was big and they were little, gave the rest of his candy to the kids sitting next to him. When Mrs. Myra nodded at him in approval, he felt like an adult.

He wandered the giant white tents with Mrs. Myra. At the games tent he saw arm-wrestling contests and cribbage tournaments, at the theater tent he watched a mermaid dance done by the high school dance club, and he perused the crafts tent housing all the nice old ladies, plus Blade, who was there every year, selling his bone-handled knives. Six dollars left, he decided against another snack and bought Mrs. Myra the prettiest wind chime he could afford, made with wire and sea glass and periwinkle shells. After he gave it to her she bought him an ice cream because he had spent all his money.

They didn't get back to the house until late afternoon, right when the rain started, and Myra took a nap while Leo and Dog snuggled in the sofa and read from the old red book. He turned the pages and, like always, saw things he had never seen. A new, brief poem appeared, one whose ink shone like it was still wet.

> *Lupine root to stamen*
> *Dark Pines anchor laymen*
> *Tighten the net right tight*
> *Guard the paths this night*

He turned the page and was surprised to see "Until the Moon, Only Then" again. It was in a different place on the page and now had more lines.

Instinct told him to wake Mrs. Myra up from her nap in her rocking chair.

"Miss Myra, my 'Until the Moon, Only Then' poem has more words!"

"Does it now? Show me." Leo led Myra to the book on its stand overlooking the windows overlooking the sea and night sky.

> *Until the moon, full, drips down*
> *After a bloodstained mackerel sky*

Until a brother for a brother, waves round
Until the lines are crossed, wayfarer by
Until a daughter for a son, both of rock, both of wave
Until the twin pearls together return,
Until a mother for a mother, one lost, one saved
Twin hearts to forever burn
Only then will the mad fog dissolve in curls
and her curse recede to the deep
What was barren shall unfurl
What was awakened shall go back to sleep
The dead will rise from their slumber
Then the mermaid shall return to the sea.

She read both poems and looked directly at the boy as the sun set red.

"Do you have this memorized?" she asked with some urgency.

"I mean, mostly? I could memorize the rest?" Leo questioned.

"Good. We need to do something with it, as soon as we can. After dinner. You go practice and I'll have dinner done quickly."

Leo had no idea what she was talking about, but she was old, and he was hungry, so he went outside and tossed sticks to Dog, chanting the poem from the book.

"Only then will the mad fog dissolve / and the curse recede to the depths / What was barren shall unfurl . . ."

He threw the stick long and far, across Myra's driveway, the twilight melding into night, and Dog chased it, a big goofy grin, tongue lolling.

And when the car swerved up the driveway neither Dog nor the driver saw each other until it was too late.

The stick landed in the grass, an incomplete fetch. Dog landed in the grass next to it, right by the maple tree that Leo hit back in March. Leo ran to his fallen companion and put his hand on his furry chest. It was moving, but rapidly, struggling. Myra rushed out and tenderly stroked his soft ears, whispering soothingly over Dog's plaintive whines. Leo thought he saw Myra's hand glow gold for a brief second, and then the gold disappeared from her hand into Dog, but it was through tears and a crazy thought, so he dismissed it.

"Dog's gonna be okay," Myra promised Leo, her hand gripping his, a promise that he needed to hear, and she needed to believe.

Then the driver of the car stepped out and puked, and Leo recognized the retchings of his mother.

"I told you I'd be back, brat. Get in the car."

Poppy, swaying, gripped Leo's arm and tried to pull him toward the car, her nails splitting his flesh, her fingertips bruising his arm. He fought her off, and then Mrs. Myra came between them, broom in hand.

"Get off my property, Poppy, and don't come back," Myra warned, steel in her words and her stance.

Poppy smirked, reached into her purse, and clumsily pulled out a gun.

"Shut the fuck up, bitch. You all are gonna do what I say."
Poppy was drunk, mean drunk, and the pills were coursing
through her misfiring system. Leo's heart leapt into his throat;
he was very familiar with this side of his mother; this was the
side that terrorized him, that hit him, that abused him. She
was off the rails and volatile. Leo realized two things that
night: One, that his mother was broken. Whether it was the
drugs or her childhood or her brain, she was a broken human,
and that had nothing to do with him or who he was.

And the second truth that Leo understood was that his
mother *would* shoot.

Leo carefully stepped in front of Myra, between gun and
broomstick, and tried to reason with the shell that was Poppy.
He thought he heard Mrs. Myra whispering something as he
begged his mother to put the gun down, her eyes red, wild.

Then the sheriff's car pulled up the drive, and Poppy would
have fired, the drugs and anger rushing to a head, but she
called out in pain as the hand on the gun snapped back, the
bones hideously broken, the weapon thrown out of her fingers.

Leo heard Myra's broom rap smartly on the ground, and
her whispering ceased.

He turned to her then.

"Miss Myra, did you do that?"

The sheriff jumped out of his car and yelled for Poppy to
get down on the ground.

She didn't.

She ran.

She ran the same route Leo ran through the Paths when he was drunk that night he tried to back out of Myra's barn on the ice and bumped into the maple tree, the same maple tree that now shaded Dog's broken body.

When the fireworks began, Sheriff Badger, Leo Beale, Myra Kelley, and the ghost of Dog were chasing Poppy Beale to High Cliffs.

Myra spoke softly, strongly:

> *Lupine root to stamen*
> *Dark Pines anchor laymen*
> *Tighten the net right tight*
> *Guard the paths this night*

Leo recognized that poem from the book. Then Leo swore he saw the Path below his feet glow brighter, glow gold, and he heard the great bald eagle Maximus overhead, flying past the moon.

Poppy got to the cliff's ledge, the end of her mascara, the edge of the world. Poppy knew that they had absolutely killed him. That pin hadn't fallen yet, but with the bowling ball of her addicted, fritzing brain, it was inevitable.

The pharmacist had just been in the way. Nothing to be done.

But there was a picture of the pharmacist's cheeky toddler tucked behind the keyboard and under the computer, the shiny surface of which was now splattered with splotches of dark red blood, and the sound of the gunshot and his sawed-off scream played on a vinyl in the ballroom of her mind and skipped and skipped and warped and skipped.

She wanted to throw up again.

She had been at the edge before, but not like this.

This could be so effortless. She could disappear like the great Captain. Like him, they wouldn't know if she fell or she jumped. She could become legend.

Her skin crawled; her broken hand looked like an octopus, puffy and purple and round in the middle, her fingers hanging off like limp tentacles. She had lost her shoes. She had lost the gun; she couldn't remember where.

Witch, witch, Myra's a big bitch, a big witch, they used to taunt in grade school. *Witch, witch, Myra's a big bitch, a big witch*, went the chorus in Poppy's head.

The sky was clear, full of endless stars and the bright thumb-print of moon.

Her heart was beating erratically; she couldn't stop twitching or grinding her teeth; more, she needed more. She stood at the edge and looked to the billows, where she saw bare-chested and bare-breasted merfolk frolicking. Their diving made her dizzy, brought her closer to the tip of the lip of the land. Her toes over the end let the littlest landslide release from the cliff's overbite and fly before being engulfed by the sea.

One of the mermaids, her tail iridescent and changing colors like a cuttlefish, began to sing. Poppy heard nothing else.

The Path was glowing gold; Leo was sure of it now. All the little rocks were sparkling, nacre; Manon's lupines and all the flowers that lined the trail were illuminated from the inside; the glow stretched out to the precipice and as far behind him as the Paths went. He saw his mother up ahead, out of reach. He knew this phase—freaking out, tweaking out Poppy. She lost her mind from all the drugs and the bipolar, which Leo diagnosed online. She was going to fall.

"Boy, say it with me. Lupine root to stamen . . ." Myra commanded, her arms glowing white from her wrists to her elbows, glowing like the Paths, glowing with the Paths. Leo didn't hesitate; Myra was his North Star. He joined her in the chant.

"Dark Pines anchor laymen . . ."

When he joined, the gold grew brighter, and when he looked back, he saw the golden Paths crisscrossing the entire landscape of Mackerel Sky, like a net set over the land, like a retaining wall.

Past the ruins of Burrbank's house, near the cliff's edge was the ivy-covered torch. Myra whispered to her broomstick, and the tip caught fire, reflecting in Leo's wide pupils. She went to the cenotaph, pulled some ivy away, and lit the top.

Sheriff Badger was running to Poppy, calling to Poppy to come away from the edge. A firework exploded.

Poppy tripped at the end of the golden Paths high above

the water, one arm reaching for the ocean like the virgin on the rocks in Mackerel Sky's oldest cemetery.

Then she fell.

The sky flashed green and blue and gold, colorful like a candy factory, when the mermaids wrapped their arms around her and pulled her under, when the sea swallowed her whole.

One Hundred Full Moons

*T*alk spread like fire across a plain when Stéphane Stowe, the Blackest man in Mackerel Sky—in fact, one of the only Black men in Mackerel Sky—returned from Florida with a white woman. He went fishing there for three winters and came back after the third with a bombshell aboard his boat. She had hair black like wet dark bark, and eyes of green that sparkled disarmingly.

They said that Millicent Stowe would have won Miss Mermaid in the Open Pageant that they held every year

Friday night at the Mermaid Festival, but she never entered. She was quiet, reserved, and preferred the library above all things. She fell into books and disappeared for hours at a time. During her pregnancy she walked the beach and read borrowed books that she shelved when she worked in the stacks. Millicent loved water and word, her husband and son.

Stéphane had not been back to the Millcreek Library in years, but he ended up there in the early morning of the Mermaid Festival. He had come into town to check on his boat and found himself with his hands in his back pockets, watching the waterwheel. The library held a book sale during the festival every year, and he had some books to donate that had been sitting in a box in his house for months, piling up, and today felt like a good day to get something done long overdue.

He waved to Widow Pines, who, although a librarian for decades upon decades, kept fisherman's hours and so had been up organizing children's books since about three a.m., before Stéphane arrived with the end of night. She hugged him, as she always did, and told him she had something for him. He followed her into the dark library to the back office the same time as the sun rose.

He remembered the smell of the library—paper pages and carpet and oranges, Widow Pines's favorite snack. He moved the rest of the big boxes of books for sale outside for her because he thought it foolish she move anything heavy herself. She thought him foolish for worrying. She fed him coffee and doughnuts as thanks and told him she missed Millie every day. Widow Pines loved books and loved introducing books to children even more so, and Millie was always akin to a wide-eyed child when it came to books, so when Millie worked at the library they got along properly.

Widow Pines handed Stéphane a journal, leather-bound, with an empty setting in the cover where a stone was once embedded. Inside the front cover, *Musings of a Mermaid: A Memoir by Millicent Stowe* was written.

"Funniest book, that journal is. I found it in the fantasy section, near the mermaid section, of all places, and kept setting it aside to return to you, and I kept on forgetting where I had put it down. Very strange. Almost like it was moving on me! But this time it stayed put. I thought you'd like to have it. I'd find her in all corners of the library, Millie; she was always reading and writing. I thought she might have something she wanted to tell you." Widow Pines patted his hand. "Your boy's gonna be fine, Captain. He's got good genes."

She smiled, nodded, still as a lighthouse.

When Blade got back into his truck he put Millie's journal on the dashboard, and it sat there while he sold his handmade knives with the bone handles in the craft tent. It sat there while he drove the half hour to the hospital to visit his son as the Mermaid Parade was marching down Main Street. Blade couldn't open it yet. He didn't want to lose himself in grief over the memory of his wife when his heart was already breaking over his son. It stayed forgotten on the dashboard through the Mermaid Festival fireworks and overnight, but then in the early-morning hours he brought it into Derrick's hospital room.

Ricky Townsend had fallen asleep; he had spent the whole of yesterday there, sitting and eating fried dough, reading poetry out loud, narrating the baseball game. He stood up as Stéphane entered and wiped his hands, covered in powdered sugar, on his pants.

"Fried dough," he apologized, his hair spiking all over the place from sleeping squished in the chair.

"Derrick's favorite," Stéphane stated, and Ricky smiled sheepishly because he already knew.

"How's the room working out?" Stéphane asked.

Ricky had rented a room owned by Gladys, Beatrix, and Agathe-Alice on the Lone Docks.

"It's really good. It's working out good."

The Three Bats had shown up at one of the baseball home games, three old ladies in their deck chairs, and at one point called Ricky over with a knitting needle.

"We heard you needed a new place to live," Gladys said to him that day.

He nodded.

"We have a spare room available. We also have an apartment that should be available very soon," Agathe-Alice added.

"Come by this afternoon, after you have visited that sweet

boyfriend of yours. Let him know we need him back on the mound," said Beatrix.

The Three Bats smiled at Ricky's shocked expression. Ricky had no idea how they knew, but he basked in the comfort and joy of being out and himself safely for the very first time. The old ladies knew he and Derrick were boyfriends and didn't slip on a stitch. Still, he tested the waters. He said quietly, very quietly, "He is very sweet, isn't he?"

"Ayuh." Gladys.

"Sweeter than sugar." Beatrix.

"Don't you worry, deah." Agathe-Alice.

Ricky's legs felt more solid on his foundation of self with their acceptance.

In exchange for pennies of rent Ricky helped out as the Three Bats' handyman and personal grocery shopper at the IGA and lived in their spare room, under the apartment where Manon lived. He had magazine pictures of David Bowie taped to his walls, a bulbous old television from the eighties, and a wastepaper basket filled with hospital visitor name tags. He wrote in his journal every night and never felt more alive. He missed Derrick achingly.

Still, he wasn't yet ready to sit and chat with his secret boyfriend's father next to said secret boyfriend's hospital bed. He didn't want to accidentally out Derrick. He mumbled some sort of goodbye and left the last of the fried dough for Stéphane or one of the nurses or anyone on his way out of there.

After checking on Derrick (no change), Stéphane sat in the mauve chair to read. It was still warm from Ricky's vigil. He opened his dead wife's journal.

And began to remember what an old spell had made him forget.

In his coma, Derrick felt like he was in the womb of the sea. Dark as night shadows and warm; he heard the continual rushing of currents like a bloodstream.

He couldn't remember how he got there.

Content, relaxed, he swam somersaults and figure-skating axels and reveled in his free body. A bubble floated up past him, then two, then a tumultuous multitude, and suddenly he was in the middle of a school of mermaids, swimming up up up to the surface. They cracked the mirror of the sea into a world of white and gray—a blizzard above swells.

"This is where you live," a mermaid of goldenrod and mustard seed gasped reverently, frightened. Derrick had never thought of it that way, that some mermaids believed that where the waves on the surface of water met the air, not the land itself, was where humans came from.

Some of the mermaids had no fear and surfed the giant crests of the blizzard with abandon, jumping like porpoises, gilded breaching. When the orca came barreling toward them, hunting, he saw his mother; she grabbed his hand and pulled him into the deep, their tails beating in rhythm, speeding mermaids pushing hard beside them, the water blooming red behind them.

They swam a long time before they switched course and began heading toward the surface and the light. When Derrick's head burst through the seawater he saw a beach beyond the billows, a beach he knew well, the beach where he practiced pitching and his mother walked every day, the beach where the Townsend twins beat him into oblivion, Mackerel Sky's Crescent.

He and his mother climbed onto a rock, their tails flirting with the sea.

"I loved this place when I lived with your father. I walked it almost every day, at sunrise, pregnant too."

"Did he know?" Derrick gestured to her tail, and then suddenly he became overcome because there she was right before him, his mother, who had been dead since he was eight. His mother was a mermaid.

"He knew at first; he rescued me. I would have died had he not taken me aboard. I was trapped in a net, ghost gear from a boat. He cut me free, took care of me. He won't remember now, of course, because that's the magic," she said sadly. "If he finds my journal he will remember, but only while the covers are open. When they close, he forgets again." She looked to the moon as if they shared a secret. "I had to leave him, and you—not because I wanted to. I never wanted to. I loved him, and you, so much. I made a deal with a sea witch to have a human life with him. I never expected to be so lucky as to have you! One hundred full moons, no more. I was only allowed one hundred full moons to be human, and in that time, during those moons, I married your father, had you. It was wonderful. I only left because the spell expired, and I had to return to survive."

She turned to the beach, where a younger Stéphane was chasing a much younger Derrick on the shore.

He remembered that day on the beach; it was the day she drowned. He remembered that day; he would see his mother's shoes and shorts by the water's edge, but not his mother.

He realized he was watching a memory.

He saw himself tumble in the sand and be picked up and swung over his huge father's shoulder, scream-laughing. He saw the two of them, father and son, at the dawn of a terrible heartbreak, running carefree on the beach toward his mother's clothes, the last indication of her they ever saw.

For months afterward, Stéphane and Derrick would each sleep with T-shirts she had left behind in the laundry hamper, waking each morning with the clothing wet from tears.

But the vision wasn't happening as he remembered it. He remembered them calling for her and no answer. And then the tragedy starting. He remembered the police and coast guard, his parents' friends' boats searching.

How a month later they declared her dead. He remembered that very well.

But this version was different, in this version his mother emerged from the ocean a mermaid, and he and his father ran to her in the water and embraced her.

"It's time," Stéphane said, a question, a prayer.

"Yes," she said.

They cried.

Tears make an ocean, Derrick remembered Myra Kelley saying to him once.

Derrick wasn't sure how, but he understood. His mother's potion, her spell, had come to its end, and she could no longer be human. His father knew. His father knew all along.

He watched her kiss them both goodbye in the past.

"The sea witch came to me that final full moon, that day I left you on the beach. She offered me a choice. She would give me a lifetime as a human in exchange for you. So the hardest decision of my life, to leave you, became less difficult in the end to make, because I would never give you to her. Me leaving meant you could live. Me leaving meant she could never touch you."

As she narrated the memory, Derrick watched his mother in the past lay her forehead on her husband Stéphane and then kiss him full on the lips. She then turned to Derrick and hugged him fiercely. Derrick saw how much his family loved each other, and that eased the yoke of his sadness.

"I will return. I don't know how, but I will. I will seek the magic out in the waters, and I will see both of you again. But until then, it is safer for you not to remember."

She kissed them once more, then swam out to the deep. She sang to Stéphane and Derrick then, a siren's song that did not have the same effect on Derrick the merman as Derrick the eight-year-old boy saying goodbye to his mother. The song was beautiful, haunting, like the lament of a falling star. Derrick watched as his younger self's and his father's eyes glazed over and sparkles tumbled out of their ears.

"Those lights are your memories of me as a mermaid," Millicent said, tears mixing with the sea spray. "Including this last one. The spell took them from you and then hid them. This last memory was hidden deep in your mind. The other memories were kept in my journal, which was concealed in the library by a misplacement spell. It will now find its way to you."

"I wish you didn't have to go, Mom." His mother embraced him on the rock in the sea, held her son in a hug that only could be given by a mother. On the beach, once Stéphane and Derrick emerged from the ocean, the memory now unfolded as it always had: they ran to the clothes first and then the water and began calling her name.

"I'm still looking for a way back. I will find it. I will find my way back to you," Millicent said, her eyes sharp.

They watched the father and son hug and cry together, and then Millicent the mermaid held her son Derrick on the black rock under the sun and they cried too, scraping off the barnacles of grief that had built up over time.

"Your father loved more deeply and more fully than I could have ever hoped for. He loves you in that same way, just the way you are. Because who you are is beautiful." She cupped his face. "How much I have missed you."

The beach was empty again. Derrick followed his mother back into the sea, and they swam until they were surrounded by the green and gray and black of the water once more.

"Why were you always writing and reading about mermaids if you were one?"

"I was fascinated by what you humans thought you knew. I wanted to know about our history through the eyes of humans. Perhaps the humans know something about my spell that the mermaids don't. But mostly I love books, learning about this surface world, which exists only in the imaginations of my kind. We don't have such things in the ocean, and to be able to open a binding and travel or fall in love or learn about history or ancestry or to fight a battle is a special kind of magic."

Derrick agreed. He too respected the power of words.

Suddenly, underwater, from above, from everywhere, the water glowed with a bright light that grew in intensity. A great golden net was descending from the surface at a pace too fast to outswim. Millicent embraced Derrick protectively, but the shimmering net passed through her body entirely like a ghost and ensnared Derrick, pulling him far away from her. She struggled to catch him; the net pulled him away too fast, and soon Derrick's mother disappeared in the dark. The net pulled and pulled, and he burst through the surface and over the town and down Route 1 and then west to the hospital, where the golden net pulled him to the corner room on the third floor past the mauve chair and into the bed and back into his body, where after six weeks and four days of being in a coma, Derrick Stowe opened his eyes.

Blade sat in the chair, reading his wife's journal, tears streaming down his face. The hidden memories of Millicent the mermaid mended the rips in his heart.

His wife was a mermaid.

And she was alive.

"Dad?" Derrick's voice was weak, thin, but it was audible.

Blade closed the book and rushed to Derrick's bedside, his heart bursting to the brim with hope. He saw his son's open eyes and kissed his son's forehead and let the tears come.

"Bonjour, mon fils. My dear boy. My love. My life." Stéphane sat on the edge of the bed and embraced his son, embraced his breathing, awake, dear son, in a bear hug entangled in hospital wires, and amid the furious flurry that followed, nurses and doctors that broke into orbit around them and ran tests and took vitals and measured the vitality of a life, the father and his son were perfectly still, together.

The Broken Sunrise

*T*he boatyard was abuzz at two a.m. when Jason pulled up. Men smoking or not smoking in hats or not in hats and all in bibs stood around truck-bed roundtables. They discussed all the breaking news in and around Mackerel Sky, from the shooting at the pharmacy in Bangor that Poppy Beale and her latest boyfriend were involved in, to Poppy Beale falling off High Cliffs after she might have murdered Myra Kelley's dog. Blade wasn't there again, he was taking another day to stay with Derrick in the hospital, and they spoke about that too. The Townsend twins were in juvie, so the port was short two sternmen, but most agreed they weren't worth a damn anyway, and what they did to Blade's boy was simply unforgivable.

Quarter to four, Oswald, Deaddeer, and the Smith boys came down under the hill and told the men not yet on the water that they had finished up at Myra's. There were a few boards left to be nailed on the barn, which the Smith boys fixed up right quick lit by the headlights of their car, and then stacked the remaining wood and cleaned up any scraps. The boy Leo had done a fine job so far, but he would be dealing with a lot bigger challenges now and the boatyard decided the barn no longer needed to be one of them.

"How's Leo? How's Myra? They find Poppy? How's Dog?" A chorus of questions from the shore boardroom.

The coast guard had mounted a search and rescue, though not a soul, including Leo, especially Leo, believed Poppy Beale would be found alive, if she was found at all. The plummet most likely shattered her spine, if not, she suffocated on salt water, if not, she was battered and bloodied on the rocks, if not, she was sucked into the sinister quicksand of a honey-pot and disappeared into where the land melted and the sea solidified.

Not to mention the possibility that the mermaids them-selves had taken Poppy to the bottom to drown and then decorate their underwater village, forever tethered to the seafloor, a rotting balloon.

"Guard's just getting out on the water now. Myra and the boy are riding home with Sheriff Badger after giving their statements at the station. Sheriff Badger's brother is looking after Dog," answered Bob Smith Jr., a descendant of Robert and Sally Smith, proprietors of the puppet show on the pier and founders of the first Mermaid Festival. Like most of the boatyard, he had been up all night and would be going out on the water to look for Leo's mother.

"No shit. Look what the cat drug in. Ike Badger. You sure?" Jason's cousin, Iggy Winslow, still pink from drink, swayed and slurred.

"Ayuh," Oswald said. "He was there when we got there, loading Dog up into his truck. I asked him if he was gonna be okay. 'Depends,' he says, nothing else. But if anyone can fix him, Badger can. No better vet in these parts."

As always, Oswald's word was worth its weight in salt. Ike Badger preferred the woods to the town and animals to people, and spoke few words, if any. He lived with two wolfhounds off one of the oldest tributaries of the Paths deep in Black's Woods, and seldom left. He was regarded as one of Mackerel Sky's resident eccentrics, an animal whisperer and healer and sculptor of uncanny ability.

"He chainsawing today?" someone asked.

In the wildwood, Ike carved tree stumps into wildlife with chain saws. He always donated one to the auction at the Mermaid Festival, though he rarely accompanied it.

"Not likely," replied Bob Smith Jr., who had seen Dog's

labored breathing and bloody, mangled leg hanging off the stretcher.

Sunday after the Saturday of the Mermaid Festival was usually a subdued one in the town; people were hungover, but many went to church, hungover or not. Many men fished, some still drunk, like Deaddeer, who would end up at the Sunday afternoon mermaid-themed library story hour asleep in the back. Widow Pines always let him be. But this Mermaid Festival Sunday the hive of Mackerel Sky had been smacked on the side with a stick and was buzzing busily to right itself.

Jason was not working today, he typically took Sundays off, but today he would be going out on the water with the rest of the town to look for Poppy. He and Manon had been planning on visiting Iledest again this Sunday, but when they were interrupted mid-coitus for the second time in their marriage bed by flashing blue lights from up over the hill, coming from Myra Kelley's, they let their plan go like a soap bubble in the sky. She was meeting him later on in the morning to help with the search; she had stayed up at Myra's to clean up her kitchen, which was in disarray after the evening's events, and Myra Kelley's kitchen was never in disarray.

Myra and Leo, carrying a large tote bag, arrived at the shore, no Dog alongside. The remaining men stopped talking as she walked up to Oswald, very tall, older than Myra by a bit, who would fish until he died. He was one of Myra and Bernie's oldest friends, a boatyard staple, another rock of the land.

"I assume I have you and"—she spoke louder to those on

the shore—"all of you to thank. Leo has been doing a mighty fine job of finishing up my barn, but we appreciate the help this morning." Oswald hugged her then, as he did when they buried her husband. When she pulled back, Myra did not wipe her tears. "Thank you all, for the flowers in the cooler. A little something for all of you." The tote bag was full of food that Myra had made just this week—divinity fudge and deviled eggs and crab sandwiches and a jug of sun tea. Leo was glad to put it down. Once he did, he immediately reached for Myra's hand. She held his left hand with her right hand, and then put her arm around him, held him steady, held him close, held him up. Every cell in her body, every hair follicle, every pore supported him, anchored him, buttressed him. When his boat threatened to float away and lose itself in the tears of the ocean, Myra's mooring chain went taut and tugged back, and Leo felt something he had never known in his life: stability. Leo was used to storms in his life, but not lighthouses.

Leo didn't know Oswald too well, but he liked how kind he always was to Mrs. Myra and how old he was and how tall he was. He smelled like the edge of the land, like seaweed, and he was always warm and had eyes that were always laughing. He'd point out all the sea creatures on the dock to Leo and the other local-kid wharf rats who played around the pier.

Manon arrived and Jason met her at the boatyard. She hugged Myra and she hugged Leo. Her hug was a good one, it was strong and solid and front and center. Leo thought that she looked rather pretty; though she had bags under her eyes from no sleep, she wasn't as skinny as she usually was and her cheeks had a little blush.

"This is right shit," Manon Perle said, and Leo respected the profanity. Then she followed with, "Dog's gonna be fine, Myra," and Myra caught Leo again while he cried out the exhaustion and worry, until its languish diminished, and then he was soothed silent by her swaying.

"Fancy a ride around the reach aboard the *Laughing Lamb*, Lorelei?" asked Oswald, removing his cap. He turned to Leo and shook his hand. "I assume that's why you are here. I'd be honored to take you aboard." He didn't finish the sentence with "to look for your mom," but everyone understood it was implied. No one doubted that when Myra Kelley and Leo returned from the police station that they would be down by the shore to hop a boat to search with the crews, no matter how little sleep they had had.

"Manon, Jason, you are very welcome too."

"You'll make room for three more young ladies, if you know what's fucking good for you," Gladys quipped, jokingly, as Beatrix rolled Agathe-Alice up beside her in her wheelchair. Widow Pines, their ride, peeled off in her truck, back to the library.

Leo's mouth dropped open; he had never seen the Three Bats on a boat before, but Oswald and Jason used the Lone Dock's forklift and transferred Bat and wheelchair to boat like they were born to it, and soon the three women were knitting elbow to elbow in the stern.

"Sistah," Oswald said and kissed Gladys on the cheek. Leo saw that she had the same smiling eyes as tall Oswald.

Oswald took her hand and led her aboard, Jason followed with Manon, and Leo took up the caboose with the tote bag, which he emptied into a plastic tote at the base of the wharf, which had been left there years ago for that very purpose—a catch-all for the treats of Myra Kelley, Bernie's dear wife, God rest his soul.

The Sisters looked at Myra. "Torches lit," they greeted, in unison.

"Torches lit," she replied.

The first light of sunrise filtered, split, and refracted through the clouds. The day bloomed a perfect mackerel sky of blue, the clouds spread across like fish scales. As the sun rose Leo noted the Paths lightly glowed gold near the precipice of High Cliffs. Leo saw, now that they were pulling out of port, bonfires and torches were ablaze up and down the coast, lights against the dark.

"A warning," said Myra.

The Three Bats nodded and then looked at Leo.

"Come here, boy." Beatrix beckoned with a knitting needle. The women were sharing one blanket between them, an ancient blue-gray quilt with what looked to Leo like cobwebs of stars sewed with gold thread. The three ladies, the oldest

Leo had ever seen, were tracing the golden embroidery with their gnarled, spindly fingers. "Oui, ma cherie, we have something for you."

Myra nodded that it was okay, and Leo stepped forward tentatively, convinced they had nothing to offer that he would want, but Gladys pulled out a king-size chocolate bar and handed it to him.

"Serious shit requires serious chocolate," she said. "We are truly sorry about your mother," she followed up, and the Three Bats nodded. Beatrix placed her hand supportively on his, and he found her hands soft and gentle like Mrs. Myra's. Old ladies weren't as creepy as he used to think they were.

"Thank you," he replied.

Leo didn't know what he thought or felt about his mother yet. Death had always orbited around her, was always right there on the periphery. She lived her life trapped in the attic of a burning building, walking the ceiling beams high as the flaming wood fell all around her. Leo had been looking for her body a long time, on the curbside couch in the trailer, by the toilet in the bathroom. She had been dead for him a long time before she fell.

The day was mild, calm, like it too was recovering from the aftermath of the Saturday of this year's Mermaid Festival. There would be an ice cream social at the church today, and more arm-wrestling and cribbage contests, and the tent would house a giant yard sale. The Smith boys would be playing their guitars later in the gazebo in the park, their wives manning the Punch and Judy show. The line for fried dough would stretch long all day before the truck packed up for the year. Leo wondered why Mackerel Sky didn't get their own fried dough food truck.

Manon was happy to be on the water leaving the town behind. The Mermaid Festival was too intertwined with the life and death of her daughter, it all still too close for her to find joy in celebration, but she could enjoy looking at it from afar, seeing the morning bustling from the safety of a boat in the harbor, an exile from the land.

But yesterday and last night, when Jason held her, some places where she had shattered began to re-form, grain of sand by grain of sand, and though she was jagged and had some hard edges in places, she was no longer in pieces, and Jason found that he mostly didn't get cut when he embraced her. And she found that when Jason touched her, her body warmed and unfurled under his hands, like a leaf to sunlight.

Manon played with her gift from the crows, Nimue's pearl earring, in her pocket; it snagged on a piece of lint, and she pulled it out to clean it. The pearl was glowing green in the palm of her hand.

Jason talked shop with Oswald while he captained, and Myra sat in silence, letting the sea air blow away the tiredness in her bones and the worries on her brow. She would return to both, but right now, on the gentle spraying swells, she could happily forget them. She was grateful to Oswald for that, and she recalled a moment when she was sixteen, back when she called him Ozzie, back on his father's boat, the *Dorothea Lee*, for the first time by themselves, her first kiss with Ozzie at the helm. That same summer Ozzie went into the military, breaking Myra's young heart, and didn't come home for four years. When he did, Myra was engaged to Bernie, and Bernie was Ozzie's good friend. They remained good friends until their final goodbyes in the hospital.

Oswald was seventy-nine years strong and would never not be in love with Lorelei Lamb Boucher Kelley, but he was smart enough not to bother her with it, especially right now, when the white sunlight was bright on her cheeks and her smile was content, the boy Leo nestled up and asleep beside her, dreaming about fried-dough trucks, his cheeks chapped with dried tears, his sleep deep.

Just beyond the reach, Iledest in the distance, a fog rose from the water, flirty wisps of silver at first, then swirls that curled and unfurled like ferns, and then grew into waves and finally thick walls of white. Oswald cut the engine as they were enveloped; Leo awoke to the stillness of the water and the air. Leo saw the fog and thought of the "mad fog" line from Ariadne Burrbank's poem in the red book.

Myra stood and pushed up her sleeves and brandished her broom. For the first time Leo noticed she had tattoos of white feathers wrapping around both her forearms, from wrist to elbow. They glowed white, light pouring out of them. She put

Leo behind her, between herself and the Three Bats, all of whom had similar tattoos and were each holding intricately carved bone knitting needles like magic wands.

Then suddenly, up through the ripples rose the curvature of a green serpentine tail, a smooth slip through the water, and then it was gone.

The sound of droplets, delicate splashes, echoed—then nothing, just breathing, and gentle waves, the water calming, like it was lulled to sleep. Then all was still.

Another mermaid tail broke the surface, this one black, the splayed web of the fin sheer like a butterfly wing. It flicked back underwater.

Myra hit the base of her broom on the boards of the boat; the brush split into two prongs, a crescent. The feather tattoos of Myra Kelley and the Three Bats, all descendants of Esmeralda Burrbank and Burning Owl, all Feathers of the Piratebird, all protectors of the lands of Mackerel Sky, flashed bright white, like sunlight on snow, like a glare on armor.

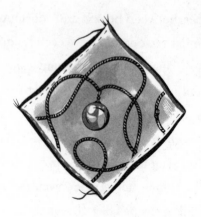

Land Sakes

Oswald kept the boat at an idle, and Jason pulled a harpoon out from below deck. The Sisters followed the gilding with their fingers more furiously, their murmurs the only noise echoing through the fog. The still water began to boil around Oswald's boat and a school of running silver mackerel broke the surface. The surge was manic; the fish were jumping into the boat. They passed starboard side stern to bow to disappear into the fog, then their splashing faded into the distance like a passing ambulance siren.

When the party looked back to the stern, Agathe-Alice's wheelchair was empty.

Immediately Jason, Manon, Ozzie, and Leo ran port and starboard to look for her, but they saw nothing but brine and brume. The remaining Bats seemingly unperturbed, and Myra Kelley not having moved from the center of the boat, the men turned back from their search rather quickly.

"She's fine," said Beatrix, following the thread.

"She's a damn mermaid," said Gladys, not even looking up from her stitching.

The water within the walls of fog swirled, whirled, erupted, shifted, became its own dynamic landscape brimming with whirlpools and vortexes and sluicing currents.

And it bubbled with merfolk.

Their tails were the colors of rocks and seaweed and deep forest flora and clouds, smooth silver scaled like tuna or speckled like salmon, striped like tiger sharks or indigo and sunshine like the blue tang. Their scales and skin colors played with the palette of the coral reef, violet or peach like the anemone, pink like the starfish, yellow and cream like the barnacle.

They dove, they glided, they disappeared deep down below. They kept their distance, but their circles around the boat tightened ripple by ripple.

Leo counted around twenty—men, women, genders he didn't recognize, varying ages too. There were three young mermaids, and Leo wondered what to call the children of such creatures. Two little ones swam next to their mothers like calves tracing whales; one suckled at her mother's breast, wrapped in a seaweed sling. The adults wore similar materials strapped and slung and over their chests in varying states of nudity. Some wore intricate bras and tops woven of seaweed and shells and strange sparkling gems harvested in the dark trenches below. Many carried knives.

One sea sprite Leo recognized. Her hair was a long cloud of silver and white and lavender, her skin alabaster. Her tail was silver and pearl, and she wore a necklace with a single glowing green pearl.

It was the one who had saved him.

He wondered if Mrs. Myra recognized her. He looked at Myra Kelley then and saw her as he had never seen her before.

Her eyes sparkling with electricity and focus, she took in all around her steadily, her feet planted firmly on the planks. She gripped her broom, its base making her a tripod. She was whispering and had closed her eyes. When she opened them, they were a fierce sharp green, unclouded. She stamped her broom against the deck three times.

Suddenly the *Laughing Lamb* began shuddering, shaking like an earthquake.

Myra stopped whispering and looked to Leo, offering her hand. "Hold on, boy."

He did.

The wood on the craft started splintering, growing new

limbs from the platform and the washboard; the transom and the coaming emerged as skinny sticks but stretched and grew into thicker and thicker branches that formed a palisade around the lobster boat's perimeter. Underwater the keel shot out sharp roots that lined up in their own paling, so above and below the waterline stakes protruded from the vessel, a floating rampart in the Atlantic.

Manon stood at the edge of the standing shelter, her heart in her throat, Jason beside her, his hands wrapped around the harpoon.

"I wasn't wrong," she whispered, arguing with all the white coats that remained in judgement inside her head, now holding her daughter's lucent green pearl earring that they took away.

"I'm sorry," Jason said. Jason, who was crying.

Manon had only seen Jason cry on five occasions in his life: when his brother died, when Nimue was born, when Bernie Kelley died, when Nimue died, and today on this boat. She turned to him then, and saw in his eyes all the understanding and love she had needed; she placed a hand on his cheek and he leaned in.

And then Manon had a thought. A thought so impossible, so absurd, so extraordinary that she could do nothing but follow it: perhaps one of these merfolk knew where her daughter was, even if it was just a tomb. She scanned the water.

The water began rumbling and shaking, and wet sand broke

through the surface in a corona around the boat and formed great mounds like drip sandcastles. Sea sirens flocked to them and lounged on the mounds like seals in the sun. The *Laughing Lamb* bobbed in the center like a bull's-eye.

Suddenly they heard Manon. The sound she expelled was a bridge between howl and wail, animal and human, sanity and madness. She held the end of the boat like she was the apex of a slingshot, moaning as if mortally wounded.

Sitting at the base of one of the magic mounds, where the sand met the sea, was a young mermaid of not more than eight wearing a kelp chemise. She had big blue eyes like her mother, Manon, and curly, unruly hair like her father.

Unmistakable, undoubtable, impossible, there was their precious lost daughter, alive, living, breathing.

"Land sakes," whispered Myra Kelley.

Manon Perle climbed over the ramparts and dove into the sea.

Jason followed, his harpoon left clattering on the deck.

Oswald would have followed, but the branches lashed out toward him, chidingly, as if the boat itself was not going to tolerate any more foolishness.

The pair swam on the midnight spoke from the lobster boat to the mounds.

Most of the fish-folk stayed back to watch the clumsy land creatures navigate the water; some mocked them openly, but all observed with great interest. Two mermaids with pink flesh and spotted tails like rainbow trout beelined for

Manon and Jason but were pushed back by a sudden swell. Behind the swell surfaced an older, beautiful merrow, her hair long and flowing and white, her skin luminescent, her tail sparkling silver.

Leo gasped. It was Agathe-Alice, who then dove immediately back under. Manon and Jason kept swimming. Another couple of mermaids sped toward them, but these two were arrested when a sudden spark of fire appeared directly in their path. They stopped immediately; their heads popped out of the water and another flame flashed right in front of them, terrifying them.

Gladys, holding her knitting needle, which was smoking a little, clucked her tongue. "I wouldn't do that shit again."

Beatrix nodded in agreement, her knitting needle sparking. "Definitely not a good plan."

Manon and Jason reached the base of the mound and pulled themselves ashore, coughing and sputtering. Most of the sea nymphs on the sand had scattered back into the ocean, but little Nimue remained in the shallows around the sand, her guardian the woman who embraced her dead daughter in the sea all those years ago.

Staring at her daughter, on her hands and knees, hand fisted around the glowing pearl, Manon added her own tears to the sea.

Out a ways, the small figure swam back and forth, curious, cautious.

"*Nimue,*" Manon called, thunderstruck. "My baby Nimue."

Something in the land-creature's voice was familiar, and the little girl's pupils flashed as foreign memories came flooding back: feeding crows from their hands in their backyard, being carried around the Paths of Mackerel Sky, seeing the ocean from the cliffs, wrapped up in a blanket on her daddy's lobster boat.

She saw her mother and remembered her, and her mother opened her arms, and her daughter swam into them. Nimue hugged her mother tentatively, unsure, but then inhaled the soft scent of mother, her mother, and snuggled closer.

All time stopped with their embrace.

Jason wrapped his arms around both of them, Madonna and child, and they held each other together. The boat was silent. The merfolk were silent. Far above the mist the clouds flitted across the sky.

Manon would have hugged Nimue forever, but she wanted to gaze upon her as she had done so often when she was little, sleeping in her crib, guarded by the nightlight. She needed to see her face. She brushed a lock of hair behind her daughter's ear. "Let me look at you, you big girl."

Her daughter smiled shyly, and Manon let out a watery laugh. "Aren't you beautiful. And so strong!"

Nimue nodded, proud, and wiggled out of her hug to swim and perform a breach backflip. She then returned timidly to her mother's arms.

"My little mermaid," Manon confirmed, stroking her daughter's brow. Jason stroked her wet curls.

Again the water rumbled, and another pile of drip sand rose through bubbles and foam, but this one was smaller, shorter, more ornate.

It was a throne. And on it sat a breathtaking beauty, lavender of skin, black of hair, and bloodred of lip, her tiger-shark tail curving regally. She wore a diadem of cowrie shells with green scintillating pearls interspersed. The water calmed and stilled.

"No need to get your feathers in a ruffle, Daughters of the Piratebird. No need to light the torches. We mean you no harm." She smiled, but Leo heard the sweet, sickly tone that his mother used when she wanted something.

Myra stood taller. "We come to ask for the body of Leona Poppy Beale. She is the mother of this boy here. We wish to lay her to rest in the ground."

Leo's stomach flipped when he heard the word *body*, but he appreciated Myra's understanding and honesty; he was sick to death of hearing how they would find her alive. He knew she was dead; everyone else did too.

The regal mermaid pouted. "Oh, we were just having a bit of fun. Some of my sirens haven't sung in so long." Her eyes flashed in warning, a reminder that they could start a song at any time.

When Myra didn't respond, the queen rolled her eyes.

"Well," she said, "perhaps I am feeling generous." She touched a green pearl necklace she was wearing with her thumb and forefinger. "A missing treasure has been returned to us."

Myra recognized that pearl. She had given it to Derrick Stowe at his mother's wake.

The queen turned to Manon and Jason and Nimue.

"She was never meant to survive on land. The water revived her." The words were direct. Mother to mother.

"She will not survive without the ocean. She cannot go back, until she comes of age."

Manon comprehended slowly, sands falling grain by grain in the hourglass of her mind until it was full, and she understood. Her daughter had been dead for four years, and now Manon had to say goodbye again. Manon remembered her own mother musing, when Manon was first pregnant with Nimue, that motherhood was a series of goodbyes.

Manon caressed Nimue's face reverently and noted with surprise that her girl still wore the single pearl earring from Myra and Bernie. It too was glinting green. Manon opened her fist and withdrew the other pearl earring that lived in her pocket, always within reach, always in her periphery.

From the boat, Myra saw the luminous viridian glow and grabbed Leo's shoulder.

"Do you remember the spell, boy?" she asked, breathless, alert, wild-eyed. Leo nodded.

Manon put the green pearl back in Nimue's ear where it belonged.

"Say it with me, now," Myra commanded.

As he said it, he saw it.

"Until the moon, full, drips down . . ."
Leo saw last night's moon, bulbous, bright, so he made one
with his hands. . . .

"After a bloodstained mackerel sky . . ."
He saw the scaled clouds, and his fingers flickered after
them. . . .

"Until a brother for a brother, waves round . . ."
He watched as Jason's brother fell overboard, as Nimuë
wailed over her brother's strangled, lifeless body, so he reached
for them both. . . .

"Until the lines are crossed, wayfarer by . . ."
He saw the glitter of the gilded Paths and opened his hands,
and it appeared in his palms. . . .

"Until a daughter for a son, both of rock, both of wave . . ."
Before Leo was the baby Tristolde, the baby Nimue, so he
cradled them, the gold dust in his palms sparkling brighter. . . .

"Until the twin pearls together return . . ."
There, in real time, under a giant drip sandcastle, Manon
clasped the earring on her daughter, Nimue. . . .

"Until a mother for a mother, one lost, one saved . . ."

He watched Nimuë rage under a full moon, men complacently walking under waves, and then Manon stitching, her head on Beatrix's shoulder, so he sewed the air. . . .

"Twin hearts to forever burn . . ."

He saw Burrbank, weathered, at the end of High Cliffs, lifting his arms to jump, Nimuë curled on her perch, and as Leo raised his arms, the gold grew out of his body and expanded in a bubble beyond the edge of the boat. . . .

"Only then will the mad fog dissolve in curls . . ."

The gilded bubble grew larger until it touched the edge of the white fog, like a yolk in an egg, and the fog dissipated in tendrils and coils once it was touched. . . .

"And her curse recede to the deep . . ."

It grew and it grew, a sphere that swelled above and below the boat to envelop sky and sea. . . .

"What was barren shall unfurl . . ."

Leo saw salmon-pink lupines aligning the Paths, bursting open with golden light, so he snapped open his hands, and a bright pulse rippled through the sphere. . . .

"What was awakened shall go back to sleep . . ."

Leo watched as Nimuë kissed Burrbank underwater, and

they swam away from Mackerel Sky into the distance and deep. . . .

"The dead will rise from their slumber . . ."

Leo heard beeping and breathing from a hospital bed, and inhaled deeply, like he was waking up. . . .

"Then the mermaid shall return to the sea."

Leo opened his eyes.

Forever a Tributary to the Ocean

*T*he fog had lifted. The water was steady, but calm. The clouds flitted across the sapphire sky like fish scales reflecting the sun, like the mackerel running slick and silver.

The sand mounds had crumbled back into the waves. The wood had retracted back into the boat, save for one arm, one thick branch that reached out port side, where Manon and Jason held on. All the mermaids dove down deep until they disappeared, leaving only young Nimue, her guardian, and the iridescent siren who saved Leo. Nimue was holding on to Manon; Manon was holding on to Nimue.

Leo was flabbergasted to see Agathe-Alice, dripping wet, back in her wheelchair. Gladys and Beatrix were knitting again, like it was a regular Sunday afternoon.

"How was your swim?" asked Myra.

Agathe-Alice preened. "Oh, just lovely. And lucrative."

The iridescent figure swam to Leo. "Hello, boy."

Leo remembered the night she saved him from alcohol poisoning. He didn't know how to officially thank a mermaid, but he thought he should, so he simply said thank you, and then quickly bowed as an afterthought. She smiled indulgently, and then inclined her head in acknowledgment.

She spoke to Myra Kelley. "The queen has granted your wish, daughter. The body has been brought to shore."

Oswald came and stood behind Leo and put his hand on his shoulder. Even though there was a sickness in his stomach, Leo had never felt so tall.

"Thank you," Leo said, and found his voice was strong.

"You are most welcome, little wizard."

She turned to Jason and Manon. "In the ocean Nimue will live. You will see her again, once, when she comes of age. You cannot look for her anymore, for you will not find her. She must travel her own current. She is like the pearls that belonged to my ancestors—once they touch land, they have to make their own journey back to the sea; we cannot seek them; we cannot find them. Nimue must make her own journey; you cannot seek her; you cannot find her."

Manon nodded, shivering. She looked to Jason, to her husband, their tears mooring them to the ocean. But two truths sparkled through their agony of separation: first, they could give up the honor of raising Nimue so that Nimue could live, that ultimately was a simple choice, and second, they would see her again.

Her daughter was alive, Mackerel Sky's own beloved mermaid.

Manon's heart breached.

She kissed her daughter's briny cheeks and forehead, her daughter's skin not sun-tanned and soft anymore like she remembered, but slick and salty, her pores now a sieve for the sea. Nimue took in her mother's embraces stoically, observant, still, tolerant but reticent, like studying fauna in the wild. The little minnow then darted back and forth among her mother, father, and guardian, emerging and receding like an eel in a reef, each time going farther, each time a little braver. She'd stop her spirited swimming to tread water, her wet eyes blinking, taking in the faces of her parents on the land, a ghost of a smile of recognition at the corners of her lips. She played with the pendant on her mother's necklace, the buttons on her shirt, the front pocket of her father's button-down. She ripped a pearlescent button off and put it into a purse strapped to her waist with kelp and cowrie shells.

Jason laughed, a watery sound, a release, a shift. "My new favorite shirt," he said.

Manon knew he meant it and would wear the shirt until it was threadbare and a hotel for moths. *My husband*, Manon thought fondly, proudly.

Nimue stayed close between them; her hands traveled her mother's face, and then her father's, like she was trying to chart the unfamiliar territory, like she was trying to see underwater.

"We love you beyond words, Nimue. Let these two pearls remind you of us, one for me, your momma, and one for your dad. We will always be with you."

"Always, pumpkin. We love you." Jason kissed her forehead.

Nimue stayed very still, nestled in the crook of her mother's arm, filling that hollow. Manon closed her eyes and imprinted the memory.

Then little Nimue slipped away, down into the dark and deep and unknown, onto her own path, where her parents could not follow. Manon watched the green pearls underwater until they disappeared.

The branch retracted back into the *Laughing Lamb*, gently taking Manon and Jason with it. It lifted them aboard, then returned to its true form of a keel. Nimue's guardian, the sole mermaid left, swam to the starboard side where Manon sobbed, held up by Jason, his arms solid.

The ocean lifted the sea sprite up, its billows framing her

prow like the figurehead that she was. She rose up on the crest of a wave like the birth of Aphrodite and placed her hand on Manon's womb. "Do not despair, little mother. You will be much occupied."

. Jason swallowed more ocean and tears when his mouth dropped open.

Then he comprehended.

"But," Jason sputtered, "it was only just yesterday, just once, well, twice, but how—" He dragged his hand through his hair and expelled a sound that was a cross between a laugh and a yelp.

Myra leaned into Leo. "Let that be a lesson, Leo boy. It only takes the once."

Leo was incredibly confused as to what Mrs. Myra was talking about. All he knew was that this mermaid floated up on waves and touched Mrs. Perle's belly and talked about mothers, and now Mrs. Perle was cradling . . .

Then he got it.

The wave receded, and with it went the mermaid, slipping into its crest, and for a moment, all were still, just breathing.

"Wow," said Jason. "I've cried more today than my entire life."

"Tears make an ocean," said Myra Kelley.

Before returning to their knitting, the Three Bats offered Jason and Manon a blanket, which the bedraggled couple took gratefully; cozied up underneath it, they were soon snoring soundly.

For the first time in lifetimes upon lifetimes, Ozzie came and stood beside Myra Kelley and put his arm around her, and the boat rocked a bit less.

Leo came up beside them. He looked at Myra. "I get most of it now, Miss Myra—but what does 'what was barren shall unfurl' have to do with being pregnant?"

She patted him on the back, and then pulled him close in a hug. She looked to Manon, snuggled in a deep sleep in Jason's arms. "I'll tell you when we get home."

When they returned to port, they were a subdued crew. They rode in silence, passing the line of shore. The fires and torches lit up and down the coast had burned down to smoke.

The Lone Docks were as busy as they ever had been, full of tourists and law enforcement and coast guard and fishermen and locals and the wharf rats and crime enthusiasts. While Oswald and Jason were tying up, the Smith boys, Barry and Bob, came running to the dock.

"They found her—"

But the elder boy's words cut off when they saw Leo.

"He knows," Myra said, and the Smith boys nodded.

"Mighty sorry about your mom, clippah," they said, taking off their caps. Leo nodded, swaying with fatigue. Then they added a burst of good news: "Have you heard? Derrick Stowe is awake!"

There was a collective shocked exhale.

"Land sakes," said Myra Kelley.

When Manon finally slept that night in her marriage bed,

next to Jason, their bodies touching all night, she dreamed of a mackerel sky.

Burrbank awoke on the highest cliff. He had slept but a few hours. The sky bloomed under placid clouds.

He had to see her again. He had to see the Mermaid.

He stood and surveyed the sea the first morning on this new, rugged coast, the waves gnawing at the cliffs, waiting for her.

Manon stepped beside him. For the longest time, the drop sickened her; she dared not, she could not go near its edge. But now she planted herself on the land and cried streams of tears that would drain through the ground to be reclaimed by the sea.

She would be forever a tributary to the ocean if her daughter could live.

For live little Nimue the mermaid did, swimming in the seas on currents, laughter bubbling, bubbling. Manon could see it, the great room of her mind, her lost daughter the mermaid.

Then in the dream she was under the water in the dark, the dark of waiting, of blood, the silence and the dark. She was herself, but not herself. She was young, little. She was her daughter that day in August on the boat, dead, wrapped in her favorite blanket, which Beatrix, Gladys, and Agathe-Alice had crocheted, sinking into the abyss. The stitched scales began to glow gold, the water began to bubble, and fish scales erupted on her legs and a tail unfurled, attached to her lifeless body. The blanket disappeared entirely into her skin, and gills appeared on her hips. And then she breathed again, deeply, violently, and she no longer breathed air.

Manon was next to Burrbank again. He was wickedly handsome, sharp edges and nimble fingers and spicy wit.

"It would not be a jump," he said. "Rather a dive. You understand. You of all."

Yes, Manon thought. *I do understand the nature of sailors leaping into the ocean in search of their mermaid.*

She cradled the growing baby in her womb. "Did you dive then?"

"A new life begun." The Captain smiled and was silent. Manon saw he was wearing a green pearl necklace.

She stepped beside him on High Cliffs and looked out beyond their world.

* * *

A few weeks later, Manon woke up and dressed at dawn. Jason was long on the water then, but his heart remained with her. She got into her car and drove past the coves under a September sunrise, the inlets carved into the land like teeth in a bite mark.

Derrick was coming home from the hospital, and the heart of Mackerel Sky beat stronger for it. She rode past lawns dotted with signs wishing him a welcome home. Four rainbow flags whipped in the wind, one in the mouth of the Crescent

Beach Christmas Pig that adorned the lone lifeguard chair. It had been dug up and discovered during the Mermaid Festival by twin boys searching for Burrbank's long-lost treasure.

Manon drove on. She thought of Nimue again, always. She flowed with the current.

Out of town, past the crimson-leaved blueberry barrens and the deeper woods, into the mackerel sky, the sun rose. She didn't want to go to the IGA to buy a pregnancy test and become the latest small-town news broadcast, so she drove thirty minutes and stopped at a pharmacy and peed on two different sticks in their employee bathroom.

She set the pregnancy tests on the edge of the sink and studied the square and circle of white where her future lay. She absolutely believed what the mermaid had told her, but she needed proof.

And on both tests a second pink line made berth.

What is barren shall unfurl, thought Manon as she cried, with a big, wide smile.

She held her secret like a seed, like a soap bubble, like a baby bird. She carried it with her through the morning, as she drove home, when she took the last two boxes out of her apartment on the Lone Docks. The Three Bats were chittering and chuckling among themselves in their rocking chairs. They spoke over each other.

"We're gonna miss you, deah," said Beatrix, and then Agathe-Alice: "How's that handsome fella of yours?" and finally Gladys: "Take this. We'll leave your damn seat free."

Manon unwrapped the bundle to a baby quilt, a lamb in a lupine field. Manon studied the intricate stitching with vague familiarity; in places the gold stitching looked like the Paths she had walked before. She looked at the three women, beautiful and wrinkled as time itself, their eyes, on her, full of sparkling mischief, their hair white and grizzled and gray and free. She hugged them each, one by one.

"Most likely a girl too," Agathe-Alice added.

"What the stars are saying," confirmed Beatrix.

"Only been wrong once," declared Gladys.

"Ayuh," the triad spoke.

When Manon returned home, she scattered two scoops of birdseed and a handful of berries for the crows. She went inside and upstairs, to the end of the hall, to Nimue's room, and stepped across the threshold.

She stood very still in the center for a long time. She ran her fingers along the spines of the books in the little library there, remembering how much she loved reading to her daughter. Hand-me-downs of *The Very Hungry Caterpillar* (which Nimue mispronounced "capertillar") and *Goodnight Moon* and *Owl at Home* and a Richard Scarry collection sat silent in shelves. She sat in the rocking chair and stared at a Dahlov Ipcar print of animals in the blue jungle.

She did all this while crying, but the tears were not a waterfall, more a steady rain that gave everything a good soaking so it could grow again. She would forever be a tributary to the ocean.

She would see Jason tonight. He would smell like the sea, and he would look at her like he did and love her like he did before they broke, and they would continue to heal. She would cook dinner with his catch, and he would ask how her day went and care about it. She would tell him about turning in her apartment keys to the Three Bats and show him her gift, and he would not understand the significance but remark on its beauty. She would tell him then that she was sure she was pregnant, and he would kiss her full on the mouth and hold her for a long time.

But for right now, for only this afternoon, she would treasure the secret of her pregnancy for herself. Later she would share her news with her circle, and the number of those in the know would grow with her belly. But not now.

Alone and not alone, she sat in the chair and rocked and read books to her womb, to her growing baby. She sketched the idea for a new quilt, a mermaid girl with dark hair, a water-rushed rock, the sunrise fireworks around her. The waves rumbled and Manon didn't hear. The pile of books and pencil shavings next to her chair grew taller. The grandfather clock ticked away time.

Volition

$\mathcal{I}$n 1721, before Torch Night when Tristolde's mother, Nimuë the Mermaid, came to Mackerel Sky and wreaked havoc on her shores, before baby Tristolde, with Burrbank his father, touched the soft sand of Crescent Beach, Boylston Townsend walked to the water's edge. He had a painful case of gout, an escalating case of syphilis, and a half bottle of rum. He had left his sweet plump wife, Brocelaide, sobbing and black-and-blue on their floor and then had been tossed out of the Ink and Crane, the tavern at the cusp of the Lone Dock and the land. He left with his jug swinging, and stalked to Crescent Beach, where he pissed into the incoming tide.

That was when he saw the thrashing merman in the net washed ashore, the verdant light of the pearl in his necklace a bioluminescent firefly. The pearl called to Boylston, charmed him. He walked toward it, listing, mouth agape. As the merman wrestled his chest free from the net and set to his tail, Boylston reached for the necklace, and the merman struck him. That snapped Boyle's nose and his temper. Boyle dove on him and smashed his pretty face into the wettest of sands, held him down where the land dissolved into the sea, and he waited until the tail stopped flapping.

He cut the necklace from the body, wrapped the body back up in the net, and pushed it back into the water. He knew those net knots, that netting; the net belonged to the Terror in the Night; he would be blamed for the death of the merman. The body floated off into the dark.

As Boylston walked farther from the water, the verdant light faded. The pearl was still beautiful, if dimmer.

When he returned home he fought with his wife again because he wanted to fight. The pearl fell through a hole in his pocket to the floor, whereupon he slipped on it and fell; his head snapped with a final crack in the angle between wall and floor.

The pearl then passed to his wife and their baby daughter, now fatherless, though that was arguably for the best. They kept the pearl content and safe and loved for many years. Time and again it glowed, usually coinciding with sightings of mermaids offshore. The pearl passed through Brocelaide's daughters to her granddaughter's granddaughter's daughter, who founded Mackerel Sky's only orphanage, the Locust House. There the pearl lived joyfully among children for a century until the house burned down, some said by witches. The stone was taken by the constable, who had it split in half to be made into pearl earrings, which he gave to his mistress, who parted with them when her house was robbed by a thief in the night. The thief was an alleyway drunkard who passed out against a wall a fortnight later, and the pearls were stolen again, this time by a barefoot boy; the pearls loved the boy and stayed happy in his pocket until he was a fisherman with boys of his own. When he died, his eldest gambled the pearls away during the war to one Bernard Kelley, who gave them to his wife on their wedding day.

"What happened to the pearl I gave you?" Derrick asked Ricky, the day he was leaving the hospital for good, leaving for home. They were waiting for his father to pick him up.

"I don't know how you will ever believe me."

Derrick cocked his head. Derrick did believe him, for he had mermaid tales of his own. He told them to Ricky. And when they were alone, he kissed Ricky. Over and over.

"My dad's here." Derrick's view from the second floor was of the parking lot and the maple trees behind it. There were pops of red among the green, those leaves diving first.

Derrick had written about it in his mother's lost journal, which Stéphane had given him in the hospital the second day he was awake. Derrick had read the journal, cover to cover, again and again—the story of his darling mother, the mermaid Stéphane rescued in the sea, and their love, and their love of him. She had left him space to add his own writing.

So he did.

fall teaches us red
in its trees tipped with winter
shows us how we die
like a sunset edging into cold
it is a forgetful season
leaves us a bit nostalgic
and mourning somewhat with crows

And he wrote:

Dock
End.
this
is where I was born
here
the ocean leaks inside by osmosis
transforming one into salt rock
white savage storm
recurring ripples

this
is where I was born
here
my ears always cold
breath always moist
cries erupting like the gulls in winter
moaning like the rigging
ceaseless attack
and recession
of sea

"I'm gonna get us coffee," Ricky said. "I'll be here, for after. I love you." He kissed Derrick, quick, full, solid. "Tell him I'm your boyfriend. I want him to know."

"I will. I love you. Here goes."

Ricky was in the cafeteria when Stéphane walked into Derrick's room. He hugged his boy.

"You ready? Duke is in the truck. We can stop—"

"Dad, I'm gay."

A reflex, the words with their own volition, and Derrick covered his mouth like he was trying to catch them. And then, "Oh shit, I had a speech."

And then heavy silence, so much so Derrick shrank under its weight. He had had a whole plan, practiced in front of bathroom mirrors and in car rides with Ricky and written down in hundreds of different ways. But his army of words ignored all strategy and stormed the field.

So Stéphane did what any good father would do, should do, and hugged his boy, his man, his son, again, because he was his son, and because Stéphane needed Derrick to know that nothing was different about him, nothing was wrong with him.

"When you were born, I was scared to hold you, to drop you. You were so precious. You were so perfect. You still are, and always will be. I love you, Derrick, as is. My son."

The strength of his son's shoulders was forged in his father's arms. They hugged for a long time; Derrick saw a single leaf flutter to the ground in a first fall.

As Derrick pulled away his dad asked: "So, Ricky, is he your . . . your boyfriend?"

Derrick smiled like a sunrise, a new day where he was now talking awkwardly with his dad about his love life, the gravitas of coming out burning off like morning fog. "He is. He wanted you to know."

Stéphane patted Derrick on the shoulder. "He's a good boy, a good man. He saved your life that night, you know." Stéphane saw his pale son in memory, his lips unnaturally blue, bloody and drowning in an inch of water. In that memory, that night would always be so dark, the only light the moon, the stars, the lights in the mermaids' eyes. He had almost lost him. How could it ever matter who his son loved?

"I know. I know about that night. I know about the mermaids." Derrick looked directly into his father's eyes, looking for a glimmer of recognition, of memory of his mother.

"Mermaids. I had heard stories, but never in my life . . ."

Stéphane's voice trailed off, lost in the disbelief. Derrick nodded, a mild defeat in a day of victory. His father did not remember, and Derrick had learned that he could not force his father to remember by opening the book with him.

He would keep trying. They would talk more. The world was so much bigger than he ever thought. His father had to remember. Myra Kelley would know how to help get Stéphane to remember. Derrick and Ricky planned to visit her in the next weeks, when summer faded in a sunset to fall. But right now he was headed home.

Ricky came in with bad coffee. As many before him, he had had a panic attack under fluorescent lights in the hospital corridor. In the past few weeks, Ricky had heard nothing from his family, which suited him just fine. He knew his brothers were locked up, and they would be for a while, which also suited him just fine.

Ricky felt and saw the relief in the hospital room but still treaded lightly. Though ready to flinch, to defend, to fight, he stood in his skin. He saw wet eyes, both turned to him. Then both sets smiled identically at the edges, and he found himself smiling back.

Stéphane drove them home along the coast in the truck as the day's colors rusted. Ricky was coming over for dinner. Derrick sat in the back, leaning against Ricky, a window open. He held his mother's journal like a bible, comforted both by its warm leather under his fingers and his mother's written words: *I promise to see you both again someday.*

He thought of his own words, how the secret of his sexuality, moored in fear, had bolted out of him so fast, as if his body could not hold in who he was anymore. And he now basked in the afterglow of the release, the relief of taking that leap. Perhaps when one almost dies for love it becomes much easier to declare it, Derrick thought, holding Ricky's hand, playing with his fingers.

Duke's head was out the window, his tongue lolling, his eyes blinking blissfully. The gentle drone of the radio and the road lulled Derrick in and out of a doze, and the coast whizzed by, sparkling, as they came closer to home.

All the Love Left to Give

"*W*ellsa," marveled Myra, holding a cup of coffee, staring out the window.

"What?" Mouth full, one of the chickens content in his lap, Leo looked too.

"Maple's turning red this year. The leaves are turning red." Leo saw a cluster of vermillion leaves in the early September green of the rest. "It's been yellow in the fall for as long as I can remember."

Leo vaguely remembered bumping into the tree that night

he stole Myra's car, apologizing to it as he ran off and then asking himself in his drunken state why he was apologizing to a tree. But today he was happy he had been kind, because apparently even trees could bleed.

"Wellsa. Ain't that something," said Myra, shaking her head above her coffee.

When he awoke that morning, he followed the grounding smells of fat sizzling, coffee, and sage smoke into the kitchen.

Myra was in her housecoat and slippers at the stove frying bacon and eggs. Four chickens were pecking under the kitchen table and at her feet. She saw Leo's look and answered flusteredly, "The linoleum's awful quiet without Dog's claws clacking on it. It was cold out this morning."

Leo greeted Dog, who was lying on a big bed in the kitchen. "How you doing, tank? Take out any cars today?"

Dog stood up on three legs to greet his best friend.

"No car accidents, but he has been trying to convince me that bacon will make his leg grow back." Myra raised her eyebrows at Dog and then tossed him a piece. Leo laughed and sat, his bed head sticking out in all directions. She put a plate in front of him and he dug in. He fed his crusts to Dog and the chickens, and one chicken, a red girl named Marley, sat in his lap, and they all settled in.

Myra Kelley's kitchen table was a good place, thought Leo.

"I can't find the poem in the red book anymore, Miss Myra. I've looked a lot."

"The spell has done its job. It's gone back in now."

"Is it gone forever?"

"More than likely. Some show up again, but that one was an agèd spell."

"An agèd spell?" Leo asked, confused.

"Means really old. Strongest magic. It's been in the book since Burrbank's time. I thought it was a poem, it was so cleverly hidden, but when it became so active, adding words, changing pages, jumping around the book, I knew it was a spell coming to fruition."

She set a second plate in front of Leo, bacon and eggs and white toast. He was ravenous and ate it all.

"Coming to fruition?"

"Means it's ready to be used. That was some spell, boy. Some spell. I don't think the town will ever be the same, in a good way."

Leo had an inkling of what Myra was talking about. When he managed the spell on the boat he had a good feeling, one of peace and contentment, like what he was doing was healing, what he was doing was right. He watched as a chicken nestled next to Dog on the bed. Dog sniffed it suspiciously, sneezed, and went back to snoring.

When Sheriff Badger pulled up a week later, Manon's crows had made a temporary respite in an arm of the great old maple that was now dressed from head to toe in crimson for the coming autumn, a flame in front of the Kelleys' hearth. He stood under the branch's red leaves admiring the birds for a moment before knocking on the old screen door.

Inside, Myra put her hand on Leo's shoulder.

"Now, boy, you and I are going to have a sit-down with the sheriff about a few things."

"Okay, Miss Myra." He liked Sheriff Badger's mellow demeanor and that he was also tall and how he spoke to Leo like he was an adult.

"I'm gonna be here the whole time."

"I know, Miss Myra."

"I see my brother has been by," Sheriff Badger said by way of greeting when he walked in, stepping around the chickens and accepting a cup of coffee.

"Ayuh. He has, left a gift for Leo by the big wooden heart on the barn."

"Huh?" Leo jumped up and ran out the door.

Earlier that week Myra had sat and chewed on her pipe and chatted with Leo as he built a lopsided wooden heart from leftover wood and nailed it to the side of the barn. Myra directed him to plant some tulip and hyacinth bulbs around the perimeter of the barn, and although Leo partially had an idea what a tulip was, he had no idea about a hyacinth, or what bulbs really were, but he did it anyway, because Myra Kelley said to.

Leo went to the barn now, to the heart, and at its base was a brilliant wooden carving of Dog, life-size, barking regally, a cape streaming behind him, ready to strike, sturdy on three legs.

"Look at this, Miss Myra! Look how cool it is—Ike must

have carved it!" Leo exclaimed as he slammed the screen door behind him, frightening the chickens.

"Ayuh, that's my brother's work right there," Sheriff Badger commented, nodding.

"Well, then, that's a gift more than most receive," Myra said. "Ike Badger isn't much for people most of the time, but he does have a way with animals. He owned Dog's mother, Leo. He gave Dog to me."

"I thought you said Dog came to you?"

Dog came to Leo then and put his head on the boy's legs.

"He did, many times. He wandered here from Ike's place, a couple miles into the woods. The fourth time Dog was sleeping on my porch, Ike came by and told me he reckoned I had a new dog. I told him I reckoned I did."

"Wait, Ike lives in Black's Woods? Like where that haunted orphanage is?" Leo was stunned.

"I don't know about it being haunted, but, yes, the Locust House is in those woods too."

"So, Leo," began Sheriff Badger, flipping a chair around and straddling it. Marley the chicken jumped and sat on his leg. Sheriff Badger didn't flinch or move to shake the bird off, and Leo counted another reason why he liked him. "You are the man of the house now. Mind Mrs. Myra, and take care of the chickens. No drinking or stealing cars. Got it?"

Leo didn't understand what he meant. He knew not to drink or steal cars. He sat quietly with a furrowed brow.

Myra sat down next to him, gently. "He means you can stay

here, Leo boy, officially. As long as you want. I'm going to be your official foster parent."

The sun rose on Leo's world.

"Really?" he asked, hesitantly, frightened, his hope a mirage that disappeared if he blinked. "Really? Not a dream?"

"Not a dream, kid. I just need your agreement, and it's a done deal." The sheriff held out his hand.

Leo looked the sheriff directly in the eyes and shook his hand like a man.

Sheriff Badger tipped his hat. "All right, then, I'll be in touch."

Later that afternoon, Myra and Leo stood in her spare bedroom, where Leo had been sleeping.

"We can clear out some of this stuff in the corner, and you can have that desk for schoolwork and whatnot, but the rule is you've got to read each of the books piled on there before you put it away."

Leo gulped at the pile of books on the desk. He picked them up and began reading the titles.

"*The Bloody Chamber, The Great Gatsby, A Christmas Carol . . .*"

"Some of my favorites," mused Myra. "I named Marley from the last one, thought the character deserved a second chance."

Leo picked up a worn, leather-bound book, full of parchment with swirly cursive writing and sketches and symbols. He opened up to the middle and watched flabbergasted as a four-line poem scampered off the page deeper into the book.

Leo turned the page, and words floated up off the page like smoke and dissipated into the morning air.

"Myra, what's this?"

"Land sakes, ain't that something! There you are!"

Leo looked around to see who she was talking to, and then realized she was speaking to the book he was holding.

"This"—Myra offered her palm with a gentle flourish, and the book jumped to her hand, and the leather string that had wrapped around it so it remained closed now wound itself around her wrist like an affectionate snake—"is my grimoire. A witch's spell book. It's been in hiding or on an adventure, I'm not sure which."

"In hiding? On an adventure? A book?"

"Ayuh. Spell books hide spells, and sometimes themselves, until they are required. Keeps them charged, kind of like plugging in a computer. Sometimes they travel to pick up new spells, but they always return."

"Is the red book a grimoire?" Leo asked, trying out the new word.

"It was Burrbank's journal at first, but it became a spell book when Burrbank wrote down a song that he once heard Nimuë sing, imbuing her song's magic into the book. It became a grimoire when it passed to the Piratebird, and she wrote down the magic she learned from witches and the Wabanaki priestess Burning Owl."

"I haven't seen any of that in the book."

"You wouldn't yet, but I don't doubt you will someday.

Because this book"—they watched as the strap unwound itself gently from her wrist and reached for Leo—"is not revealing itself to me. It showed up here, right now, the moment this became your desk, because it wants you to read it. Which means I need to teach you."

"Teach me what?"

"Magic, boy. Magic."

Dog barked in agreement.

"Indeed," Myra Kelley said.

"Miss Myra . . ." Leo hesitated. "Because we can do magic, is there anything we can do for my mom?"

Myra sighed, deeply. Myra cried then. Myra was a good griever.

"No, honey. Nothing to be done, with or without magic."

Myra held Leo as the dam broke.

Leo knew who his mother was. He knew how little she cared for him. But still he grieved. She was his mother and the concept of mother at the same time, and he grieved for what he needed versus what he got. As he cried, he felt like he was really mourning the lost possibility of having a birth mother who loved.

"Tears make an ocean," Myra Kelley said.

"Life's just one fucking tragedy after another, right?" Leo said, watery, and Myra laughed with Bernie in her heart. She kept her arm around the boy, the gentle boy who plowed right into her doorstep drunk on coffee brandy.

"Sometimes, kid. Sometimes not."

After they had their supper of haddock chowder, the fish fresh from the cooler fresh off the boat, they walked the Paths with Dog, the stars speckling the sky. They still walked the Paths every day, not after dinner like the summertime, but before dinner, in the waning light as the air grew chilly.

"How do you deal with it, Miss Myra?" Leo had a long stick and was slicing at the heads of the Queen Anne's lace along the side of the Paths.

"With what, boy?"

Aubergine was blooming on the horizon when they arrived at High Cliffs.

"The sads. About when someone dies." He said it, and the hiccupping sobs tumbled out right after. Again, Myra held him until they receded.

"Well, you do that, Leo dear. You cry, you talk, you let it out. Those tears are all the love you had left to give. Grief is all the love you have left to give. So you let it out. Love will always connect you to those you lose." Her voice broke as she thought of her Bernie, his warm palms, his crinkles at the edge of his eyes, how he winked at her when he was joking. How he would have loved this boy.

She looked to the first stars of night. "You know," she added, "Bernie also used to tell me that sometimes you just need to go to the top of a hill and yell. That helps too."

Leo laughed, and then nestled back into a second hug.

"Thanks, Mama Myra," offered Leo.

Myra felt butterflies in her heart.

"That sounds good, boy."

They stood there for a while as the word *mother* settled in the skin, and Myra hugged the boy for every mother's hug he had lost. Then they walked toward the sky, and stood at the cliff's edge, where the Sea Captain lost his heart to the siren. Myra let out a bellow, a yell that catapulted out of her body and disappeared into the horizon. Leo, wet eyes wide with wonder, belted a follow-up something fierce, his voice and his tears lost on the wind.

That night the mermaids remained in the deep. The waning September moon tilted her head toward the seaside buildings of Mackerel Sky, the Lone Docks, the crisscrossing net of the Paths, the High and Low Cliffs at the points of Crescent Beach, the night's dark enveloping one side of the moon's visage like a veil, the folds obscuring one eye.

Acknowledgments

First of all, thank you, dear reader, for picking up this little story and bringing it to life by reading it. There are so many wonderful things that we can spend our precious time on in this universe, so I am humbled that you would devote some of your time to my words.

I have been in love with theater, dancing, choreography, and writing my entire life, and they plait together creatively, influencing each other in my art. I play with words, let them dance, view the space of the page as a stage. I blur lines between poetry and prose. It takes a special type of literary agent to take on a debut author with a unique writing style like this, and I am so thankful for you, Ms. Jennifer Weltz, for choosing to represent me. Your literary ideas and knowledge, guidance, tenacity, and brilliance have, quite simply, made my lifetime dream come true. Thank you also to Cole Hildebrand and all at the Jean V. Naggar Literary Agency for the work you do for new books and authors: I so appreciate you.

Thank you to my editor, Mr. Adam Wilson (also thank you to his wife and two daughters), for the time he spends working on my novels! Thank you for believing in my story, and in me as an author. Your literary insight, patience, support of my art, and kindness during this very new process have been invaluable to me. Thank you also to Olivia Zavitson, for supporting my book from the onset, and to the edits and eyes of copy editors and sensitivity readers.

Thank you to Hyperion Avenue; I am honored that you published my debut.

A book, from muse-spark conception to hardcover delivery, can be a long process, a lifetime within a lifetime, and there are many people along that path who help you, who inspire you, drive you to write, pick you back up after rejection after rejection.

To Mummawulf: Here's to more mad teas and story ideas that won't shut up in the middle of the night and communing with the owls and faeries. And more writing. Thank you for you, but also for our writing work together, our discussions, your thoughts on my words.

To the original mermaid Michelle, ma belle Brigitte, and Jessica Jane, CaraBOSSe: Thank you for the symphonies that are you, but also for our years and years of weekends and weekends of creating and performing dance shows, and so many hold-you-up hugs, and so much laughter.

To the dancers and choreographers and performers of Vivid Motion, our innovative and kinda quirky Portland dance company: Thank you for twenty years of creative storytelling and dance and vulnerability and joy and friendship. Your art influences mine. Here's to more shenanigans and killer robots and brush-waltz balancés and pasty mishaps. #XOVIVMO

To my childhood, my family, and the town of Jonesport, Maine, where I used to run wild through the lupines visiting my cousins and my Nannie and Gramp for the Fourth of July lobster-boat races. Thank you to residents Aunt Sue and Uncle Bud, Aunt Pam and Uncle Chris, and my cousins Jay, Clark, Sara, and Zachary, for everything—your boat rides, your stories, your open arms. To the Maine lobstermen: Thank you for all that you do.

To Joseph Charnley, Annemarie Orth, Caitlin LeClair, and all the teachers at King Middle School: Thank you for what you do for students. Thank you for all your support of me, my art, and my family through the challenging times, especially recently, as schoolteachers.

To my middle school students over the years: Thank you for always believing in me. Remember: I'm so proud of you. The world needs you at your smartest and best selves—and THE WORLD NEEDS YOUR ART. Also, hedgehogs are still ridiculously cute, I miss you all, and #fenchklass.

To my bestestestestest, Celeste, forever enchiladas and scratching poetry out by candlelight lakeside and Lord of the Rings: I love you to pieces until you are whole. Find the Tori reference.

To my sister, my Jenny: You are truly one of my heroes. Front and center, a fighting heart and fierce love for all. Here's to more adventures with dogs and guacamole. I love you. Thank you for you.

To my Mommabean and Dad: My goal is to find as many public opportunities to express what amazing parents you are to the world. I've told my friends, and the Facebook, and shared it during a curtain speech, now comes the acknowledgments section of my novel. I'm excited to see what comes next. I love you both so much, and would never be here without you or your support of the artistic, sensitive human that I am.

To Eowyn, my rainbow baby: You were the miracle when we needed one, and the miracle we didn't know we needed. Introducing you to the bigness of the world and watching you interact with it is one of my greatest joys. I love you so much.

To Saoirse, my firstborn, the brilliant, talented girl who honored me with the moniker "mother": Watching you become the woman that you are is the greatest story I could ever imagine. You are a force. I love you so much.

To my husband, Bruce: All is love, especially this. In the end we all become stories, and I am so lucky that mine has been such a love story with you.

Finally, thank you to my muses, and magic, and deep-forest faeries, and sunrises under mackerel skies, et à Leon Werth quand il était enfant. The world needs your art.